BOLLINGEN SERIES XLV • 5

The Collected Works of Paul Valéry

VOLUME 5

Bollingen Series XLV • 5

PAUL VALÉRY

IDÉE FIXE

Translated by
David Paul

With a Preface by
Jackson Mathews
and an Introduction by
Philip Wheelwright

BOLLINGEN SERIES XLV • 5

PRINCETON UNIVERSITY PRESS

Princeton and Oxford

Published by Princeton University Press
41 William Street, Princeton, New Jersey 08540
99 Banbury Road, Oxford OX2 6JX

press.princeton.edu

GPSR Authorized Representative: Easy Access System Europe - Mustamäe tee 50, 10621 Tallinn, Estonia, gpsr.requests@easproject.com

First published 1965 in England by Routledge & Kegan Paul Ltd.
New cloth, paperback, and e-book Bollingen Recollections editions, 2026

Cloth ISBN 9780691292878
Paperback ISBN 9780691292861
ISBN (epub) 9780691298948
ISBN (PDF) 9780691292854

This is volume five of The Collected Works of Paul Valéry and the seventh volume of the edition to appear

CONTENTS

IDÉE FIXE

A Duologue by the Sea

Preface

VALÉRY had a particular fondness for men of the medical profession; he admired them and he liked their company. Conversation with an intelligent doctor could spur him to some of his liveliest talk. He was learned enough in the physiological version of the human being to make use of medical terms in his own speculations, and so brought a practiced imagination to the doctor's game of lacing technical ideas with amusing obscenities. At this sort of play, he had the advantage of surprise, being a "pure" poet. Also a bit of a hypochondriac, he had the heady pace of the keenly engaged.

As a physician's first concern is with the functioning of the body, Valéry's was with the functioning of the mind, and he was very clear on the connections and differences between the two disciplines. Once in addressing a congress of surgeons and wishing to give a personal turn to a formal compliment, he drew a distinction between the poet's profession and theirs. It was one of his great talents to know how to praise. "How could this mark of your friendly esteem," he said, "fail to be highly agreeable to a man whose occupation is entirely intellectual, whose productions cannot be tested or proved by any fact, and are therefore worth whatever you will; whereas you gentlemen are men who know something for certain, who can positively do something, whose thoughts and actions are proved in their consequences. Yours is one of the most complete of all professions; it requires the presence and participation of the whole man. The masterpieces of your hands are the only ones I know that can be valued in two ways: admired by connoisseurs and blessed by countless others."

The elegant objectivity a surgeon requires of himself in his dangerous dealings with the substance of life at the edge of death—this particularly impressed Valéry's imagination. He thought that the greatest human elegance is realized when supreme skill (a surgeon's, a gladiator's) involves in its performance the ultimate terms. Something of this is evident in an inscription he once wrote in a book for a surgeon friend —actually Henri Mondor, to whom the *Idée Fixe* is dedicated: "O Therapeutist, for whom the deepest viscera have no secrets, your hands, guided by the gods into the abysses and labyrinths of life, fight against death behind its bloody mask with only a pure blade and knowledge—from your mind to your fingertips. . . ." A man who from head to toe or head to fingertips is every inch knowledge: this for Valéry defined that *total ability* which is supreme skill.

When two intelligent friends, of the same sex and different occupations, are freed momentarily from the demands of work and happen to meet in the liberal presence of the sea, they have found the right circumstances for perfectly idle and sensible talk. This is the situation Valéry has provided in the *Idée Fixe*. The book is a conversation between two men who meet by chance in a quiet spot on the seashore. They are on vacation and therefore bored; they need to talk. One of them is a doctor, a surgeon, of the plump and lively type. He has brought along a fishing line and some brushes and paints, something to occupy a surgeon's hands while his mind wanders.

The other arrives; high-strung, spare, rapid of speech and movement, feverishly nervous. Boredom drives him to think, and he has been trying with no luck at all to interrupt the excited activity of his mind by walking over the worst terrain he can find. This is obviously Valéry.

Not only the whole manner of the man is Valéry but the dialogue from first to last is a repertory of his favorite topics. "The whole blank family," as he says, is here, giving us a glimpse of what he called his "System." Most of these are among the ideas developed exhaustively in the Notebooks, and at least one of them, the Implex, is here given a richer development and, by a sort of sustained indirection, more imaginative body and depth than anywhere else in his writings. Here too are the favorite butts of his destructive analysis: the "universe," the "subconscious," history, "profound" ideas, sex, Pascal, dreams, etc.

But the occasion is not one for taking these or any other ideas *seriously*. Everything here is lightly turned. This is conversation for its own sake and a virtuoso performance, a display of intellectual fireworks for the fun of it. By a great piece of luck, we can listen to Valéry talking with Bergson about the book, at the moment of publication: "Pentecost [1932]. At Bergson's, at 3 o'clock. He was expecting me. The *Idée Fixe* in front of him—with slips of paper inserted here and there. Compliments on the book. I explained that it's an *Alimentary Farce*, which amused him. He said I should have used that as a subtitle. We spoke of what I say in the book about the orgasm—that acute pleasure so much like pain, and so near it—and I counted up the critical muscular states comparable to it which characterize the *rarer* forms of elimination: vomiting, childbirth, etc. We talked about the strange economy of the body which uses the same organs for very different functions. And he said: nature has found no way to avoid using the same organ for love and urination. I replied that she economizes on drainpipes!" Etc.

The whole tone of this *Farce Alimentaire* is unmistakable. Valéry tells us that it was written in haste and he puts the responsibility for this on his publisher. But what seems just as likely is that he wrote it "off the cuff" with the idea of portraying himself talking, for it is clear that this dialogue is a self-portrait. Valéry liked drawing or painting his own portrait. Sketches of himself are found here and there throughout his letters and Notebooks, and two or three still hang in his study. Much of his writing too is a kind of self-portraiture. *Monsieur Teste* and the Faust plays contain fairly full-length studies of himself, but the *Idée Fixe* is the least disguised and most deliberate of them all. More fully perhaps than anything else he wrote, it gives a sense of the man, his physical type, his temperament, the quick natural pace of his mind, his tone in man-to-man conversation, and his notion of himself as a sort of Robinson Crusoe of the intellect, inventing his own "tools," which is to say his own terms and problems. The closing pages are an actual character sketch of himself.

There was nothing Valéry liked more than talking, and it was his natural habit to speak in a rapid mutter. His friends, even his family, complained of this. Degas, invited to dinner, would thump the table and bellow: "Valéry, stop muttering!" And Gide had known him for thirty years when he wrote into his Journal: "I have to ask him to repeat one out of every four sentences." Imagine Valéry reading the *Idée Fixe* aloud to Gide—straight through, probably, at top speed

—as he did once when he had just finished writing it: "Gide came to dinner last night. I talked to him about the 'Goethe' —an official chore—and then read him the *Idée Fixe*: Awfully tiring. We were back in our old intimacy of thirty-five years ago. He left at one. I was exhausted."

He doesn't tell us what condition poor Gide must have been in when he left, but he does warn us in his own preface that "speed is the essential." This may seem an odd notion to English and American readers who do not speak French, or even to those who do. Our pace in English is usually more casual. We incline to hesitate or reflect as we talk, and we can tolerate even a considerable pause while the search for the right meaning, or the right way of putting it, goes on. We like talk that comes from deep down, and we expect our geniuses to stammer as a sign of the profound origins of what they say. As for French conversation, whether we understand it or not it usually strikes us as unnecessarily fast, and we are likely to feel that nothing very serious is being said since nothing very serious could possibly be thought at such a rate.

The French, on the other hand, have little use for our leisurely pace or for our notion of profundity. For them intelligence is the expert use of language. To be intelligent is to be quick with the right words—*repartee* is not a French word for nothing. Slow or hesitant speech in French can easily raise doubts about the quality of one's mind. A foreigner may be badly disconcerted to find that in speaking French, if he hesitates for a word, his listener will either break in or—worse—show some disagreeable sign of sympathy for his plight.

In the matter of profundity and rapid speech, as in most matters, Valéry was traditional. He once said to André

Maurois: "I have often noticed that on most subjects I say pretty much what everyone else says. But people think it is different because my form and vocabulary are not theirs." For him an idea was profound only if no one had taken the trouble, as he said, to make it superficial—that is, to express it in precise language.

The conversation that follows should be imagined, then, as proceeding at a fast French clip. It is a brilliant singles match, as Mr. Wheelwright says, in the game of thinking aloud.

JACKSON MATHEWS

Introduction

The present dialogue, now offered in English for the first time, has received little previous attention from Valéry's many commentators. Maurice Bémol, for instance, in his two illuminating volumes, *Paul Valéry* and *La méthode critique de Paul Valéry*, does scarcely more than mention it. No doubt a reason for the neglect is that this "improvisation," as Valéry calls it, has seemed rather slight and wavering as compared with those two sturdier achievements of formal dialogue, "Eupalinos" and "Dance and the Soul," each with a clearly defined subject. When Valéry, in a characteristic gesture of self-effacement, declares *Idée Fixe* to be "a light-hearted game," we should not overlook his qualifying reminder of the kind of game it is—a game of conversation, and not just anyhow, but as an echo from the days when people conversed well. This improvised conversational vignette has the advantage of being more relaxed in tone than any of Valéry's other experiments with publishable dialogue, and it permits the speakers—the Valeresque ego and the medical alter ego—to glide easily and unself-consciously from theme to theme and from aspect to aspect without requiring a logician's passport for every change of position. There is no Socrates to dominate the discussion and craftily shape the theme. The contest is a nearly equal one, and if the "I" enjoys some slight dialectical ascendancy over the Doctor, it is in no way decisive—nothing like the clear-cut referee's decision that Plato usually expects us to award the midwife's son. Midwifery is unilateral, but in these pages we have a genuine give and take of burgeoning ideas—a friendly wrestling match between nearly equal contestants—the seeming freedom of a pair of dancers moving in rhythmic complementation. *Idée Fixe* is not quite actual conversation, but something better: it is a poetic mimesis of conversation as an archetype of relationship between two independent and vivacious minds.

Recalling Aristotle's remark that a poetic mimesis is more philosophical than a recording of actual events, let us ask in what sense the present dialogue is philosophical. More generally indeed, how is Valéry's philosophy to be distinguished from the systems that have traditionally borne that label? I do not find him mentioned in any prominent account of "the philosophies of our time," and it is rare to meet a professional philosopher, in America at least, to whom he is more than a name. Perhaps this is due to the fact that Valéry's own philosophy, or (what is nearly the same thing) his attitude towards philosophy, is so manifestly free from professional ties, so healthily remote from the lectern and the chalk box. It is the philosophy of a self-dedicated amateur. "Dare I admit," he writes in *Orientum Versus*, "that the word *philosophy* seems to me magical if I hear it innocently, far from any thought of schools? I find a charm in the word itself—the charm of some very beautiful, calm Being who can transform love into wisdom or wisdom into love." But magic, to produce real effects, needs preparatory discipline: does not Hindu legend assure us that Prajapati, in order to create the visible universe, "practiced austerities"? Philosophy for Valéry, then, is not so much doctrine as regimen—a kind of intellectual athleticism, flexing the mind's muscles and focusing its sights, "forcing that amazing machine, the human body, to produce at each moment a new and particular adjustment that demanded the utmost concentration of . . . its most contradictory faculties." To philosophize is to be always on one's toes, poised and equipped for action and inaction alike. Hamlet's cry, "The readiness is all," and Valéry's own adage, "Travel light!" epitomize this primary imperative of the Valeryan muse.

Athleticism, being so little concerned with systems as such, tends to produce a philosophy of paradox, of ambivalences, of radical plurality and shifting dialectic possibilities. Neither in the macrocosm nor in each minuscule of mind does anything stay fixed. Hence arises the very question from which the dialogue takes its title. Like Heraclitus and Hegel and William James among others, Valéry denies that an idea is ever quite the same on two occasions of its occurrence. An idea can't be fixed, Ego argues, for it is mental, and every mental state is transitory. Some ideas, to be sure, have the property of reappearing to consciousness more often than others; their appearance may be relied on in appropriate contexts; thus they are "fixed" in the sense that a roulette wheel can be fixed. They are privileged. And their privilege is shown not only in the frequency of their reappearances but also in their status—all other events, sensations, and ideas seeming to be infringements of, or at least deviations from, the mind's dominant mode of transition. For it is the nature of an idea to intervene in the mind's normal state of disorder and inattention—which is to say, in its sheer ongoing succession of images and reactions uncomplicated by any affinity of meaning—and to accentuate and momentarily arrest, or rather retard, some element in it. The idea *is*, in fact, this momentarily favored element, which, by thus being as it were coagulated from the general psychic mass, suggests comparisons and hypotheses, whereby the animal flux of images and instincts becomes transmuted into thinking. When the arrestation becomes habitual and the same idea returns repeatedly in a variety of mental situations, we have what is called a "fixed idea." But the epithet is inaccurate, as Ego seemingly demonstrates when he cries: "Look: consider yourself! . . . Can you fix an idea? You can only think in terms of modifications. If an idea, as such, remained constant, it would no longer be an 'idea.' "

At first sight it may look as though Valéry has fallen into the familiar error that college philosophy students soon learn to refute, of confusing "idea" in the sense of mental event with "idea" in the sense of meaning. A meaning, as Aristotle explains in the third book of *De Anima*, is not a mental event but a permanent possibility of mental events of a certain type to become actualized. Of course we can't think except by modifications, even in mathematics; nevertheless the mathematical idea of duality, for instance, is strictly unchanging, even though the mental modifications given to it by a lover and by a hermit will doubtless show lively differences. As Aristotle would say, the laws of whatness are one thing, the laws of knowing what's what are another.

It is a mistake, however, to confound Valéry's handling of any problem with an ordinary textbook formulation of it. He has a gift—developed and refined through years of psychic privacy won by daily attention to a job—of contextualizing freshly everything he touches. With respect to the present problem he would not deny, of course, that the mathematical ideas of one, two, three, are self-identical; the point is that he interprets such self-identity functionally. Mathematical ideas have the virtue of being perfectly reliable, subject to recall without variation in the one respect that matters most—their relations to other mathematical ideas. Mathematics is the roulette wheel that always turns up the number the croupier expects. This perfection, this precision of logico-mathematical relations, however, is unique. Other ideas—which is to say, the vast majority of ideas that men must live by—can be shaped into a loosely comparable order only at a cost. An order bought too cheaply is an order of bias, not of reason. The card-catalogue type of mind, when it grapples with problems of a human order, is quite as liable to confusion as any other—even more liable, Valéry would say. Real order has to be fought for, out of antecedent and circumambient disorder. The psyche's quest is conditioned by something analogous to the law of entropy in the physical world: there must be "a heat differential" in order for any mental work—i.e., any work of ordering—to be accomplished. And this heat differential must be boldly recognized. Everyman, like Dante, must button up his fears and "go by another way," peering into all the circles and pouches of his private inferno before the guide and authority that is reason can lead him to the mount of accomplishment. Valéry's problem, a secular modernization of Dante's, is to conquer the Absurd (always "lying in wait"), and this can be done only by accepting, assimilating, and dominating it—by deliberately exploring a wilderness (the broken rocks on the shore, "the total disorder") in which not one step, not one co-ordination of efforts, resembles any other, and hence not one can be conceptualized twice in the same way. Thus Valéry's denial of the *idée fixe* is no mere textbook solution to an epistemological conundrum; it is a first step in the philosophic task of establishing an equilibrium of moving ideas by virtue of which it is possible to think and, in human terms, to live.

But if the *idée fixe* is rejected, what principle of unity, precision, intelligibility even, is possible? The answer must be found partly in terms of sensibility, partly in terms of act—those two major complementaries of Valéry's aesthetics and, overlapping it, his theory of knowledge. The role of sensibility in his philosophy may be usefully studied by a comparison, for both likeness and difference, with Kant. Like Kant, Valéry affirms that whatever harmonies, unities, and totalities we find in the world must somehow reflect the character of the "I" that beholds them. What could sound more like an echo from the *Critique of Pure Reason* than his statement, in the essay on Poe's *Eureka*, that "All the diversity of my visual perception is harmonized in the unity of my directing consciousness"? And again like Kant, he regards this unity as functional rather than metaphysical; not so much a unity as a persistent urge to unify. But from there on the two philosophers follow different paths. The Kantian ego—that pure transcendental principle of unification and discrimination operating impartially upon all incoming experience in the very act of receiving it—is too bloodless for Valéry's more realistic and concrete temper. The difference of temper may be observed, for instance, by comparing Kant's carefully abstract deduction of the categories of human understanding with Valéry's analysis, in the essay just cited, of the actual way in which I see the world around me as a whole—"always enveloped by all the *seeing-movements* of my body, which are transformed one into another and which irresistibly take me back to the same central situation." Kant does, to be sure, acknowledge the role of spatial, hence visual, imagination in *representing* the categories to ourselves mentally. But for Valéry, who repudiates the strait-jacketing of thought by categories, the activity of vision is all-important. The Whole by which I think myself surrounded is that which exhausts my capacity for seeing; it is sight, pre-eminently, that contributes to one's consciousness of simultaneity, which is to say, of unity made manifest. Even in their manner of rejecting, the two philosophers display a characteristic difference. The idea of an all-enveloping universe, which Kant explains as a "transcendental ideal of pure reason"—something our reason cries for, like the baby for the moon, but can never reach—Valéry dismisses more brusquely as a mirage of vision. The visible totality that surrounds me, he argues, combined with the unifying agency that springs from undiscoverable depths of my mind, suggests "the image of a solid to which all my perceptive life is attached, as is a sea anemone to its bit of shingle." But can there be a shingle outside of which nothing else exists? "How can we form a concept of something that is opposed to nothing, rejects nothing, resembles nothing"?

It is in act, even more than in sensibility, although the two are inter-knit, that the unity, precision, and intelligibility for which the human mind naturally thirsts are to be found. In "Eupalinos," Socrates the Architect is made to say: "it is in acts, and in the combination of acts, that we ought to find the most immediate feeling of the presence of the divine, and the best use for the part of our strength that is unnecessary for living, and seems to be reserved for the pursuits of an indefinable object that infinitely transcends us." *Im Anfang war die That.* What does the creative act involve? The typical act, the *eidos* of all other acts in so far as they are acts and not just expressions of the disease of activity, is that of construction, of composition. In artistic—which is to say, authentic—composition, there is somehow a right mingling of inspiration and intelligence, of spontaneity and "conscious constructions and repairs" (*reprises*). The intellect must be ready to take over when the Muse yawns; or, as Valéry puts the matter in his "Reflections on Art," the original quality of spontaneity, which appears only occasionally in the course of the creative act, must be re-created by conscious synthesis, so that the author works, much of the time, by imitating himself. In this respect the author is his own best critic—not in separate exercises of criticism but in the appropriate expansion of the creative act.

Now an act, as Valéry intends the term, is by no means a mere occurrence (*évènement*). In the "Reflections" he locates the notion of occurrence par excellence in the domain of physical science, where it "is represented by a group of quantities . . . considered as simultaneous and assimilated therefore to a point—to a point-occurrence"; and where the time variable, too, is conceived as originating in a point—i.e., a temporal zero. In physical science, therefore, the notion of origin implies an indivisible point-instant-event. Quite other is the case in the domain of real creativity. The area (not the point) of departure is where sensibility and act are one, like the concave and convex of an identical curve. And in the present dialogue Valéry expresses this sort of capacity by the happily coined word *implex*. There are implexes at various levels, to be sure. Thus a muscle "can do only two things: stretch, or contract"; the implex of the retina is to register a limited set of lights and colors. An intellectual implex, on the other hand, is exceedingly more complicated, involving a tendency to make the greatest possible number of connections and fertile associations and to establish a significant tension among ideas and questions that display maximum presence and suggestiveness. For, as Ego remarks, "there's no such thing as a mind at one with itself. It would be a mind no longer." The same idea is expressed in ironic inverse when Valéry's Faust taunts Mephistopheles: "You are locked in Eternity, my dear Devil. . . . And so you are without thought. You don't know how to disbelieve, how to look for what you haven't got. Fundamentally you are very simple." *Implector ergo sum*! For to be, in the context of the Intellectual Comedy to which all of Valéry's writings diversely subscribe, is to exercise intelligence—*esse est intellegere*—and the greater the intelligence the more variously will it be interconnected (*reliée*): "its amplitude is but the high degree of its connection" (*Variété IV*). Thus at the opposite extreme from the simplistic Devil stands not the God, but the ultimate Man as described in the essay on Leonardo: "whose activities are so diverse that if I postulate a ruling idea behind all the activities, there could be none more universal." A Leonardo, a Shakespeare, a Goethe, possesses greatness—is *übermenschlich* in the true, not in the parodied Nietzschean sense—to just the degree that he is superabundantly implexive.

A poem, too, may be said to have, or to be, an implex. When a poet uses an epithet in an unaccustomed syntactical relation, what effect does it produce in the fit reader—i.e., in one with a congeneric implex in himself and ready to accept the proffered gambit? By bringing the diverse elements together in a special way—by what Sr. Vasconcelos calls a "unification of the heterogeneous"—the poet, says Valéry, has engendered a kind of special energy in whoever is susceptible to it, an energy arising from the modification of the normal semantic potentialities of words, and has thereby elicited a real creative act on the reader's (or hearer's) part. Words, like persons, can forfeit their implexive potentialities and go dead; in their ordinary use, Ego declares, they are "the creation of habit, and they cannot be used as guaranteed elements in any accurate mental construction or operation without their making it null and void." When the Doctor retorts that precision applies to solid bodies, he is falling into that characteristic and radical fallacy of so many scientifically oriented thinkers: an oversimplification of the idea and problem of precision. The precision that relates to solid bodies is a precision of denotation—of being able, in the last analysis, to point publicly at what is meant—and, in its scientifically more refined form, a precision of measurement. The static use of words, whether ordinary or highly technical, represents the attempt to capture and represent such precision by language. What Valéry, on the other hand, means by "perceptive usage" (*l'usage délicat*), the employment of words in the "service of any strict intellectual inquiry," is something essentially different, despite occasional points of coincidence. For the poet's task is to rescue language from its everyday shackles and to coax it into expressing with maximum adequacy the Implex of implexes that is the world—the flowing wholeness of things, its qualitative individuation, its protean transformations and *doubles entendres*, and above all its mocking ambiguous relationship with the human imagination and intelligence bent on trying to know it. Language is no dray horse here, but Pegasus bridled and soaring.

Three corollaries of the doctrine of implex remain to be noted, for they keep reappearing, overtly or implicitly, in so many of Valéry's writings. An implexive intelligence, by being most intricately connected (*reliée*), is most fully released and liberated (*déliée*); by assimilating the most diverse elements into its own creative life, it is most pure; and by acknowledging and accepting its inevitable relativity to material conditions, it becomes absolute. The three clauses express not three separate conundrums, but the single underlying Valeryan paradox in triple perspective. The paradox becomes luminous enough when we take care to understand the determinant words in their appropriate sense and context. Connected how? In one passage "a mixture of natures" is identified with impurity, and in another this equation is applied to practical politics—that confused jumble of "bestiality and metaphysics, might and right, religion and selfishness, science and histrionics, instincts and ideas," which tends to destroy the poised absolute that is the self's integrity. But mixture of natures is one thing, controlled acceptance and interrelation of the widest variety of experiences are another. Valéry is speaking not of the compromiser but of the man of concentrated intelligence and consciousness dedicated to the utmost clarity when he says: "The more relationships [such a consciousness] absorbs, or endures, and the more closely integrated it is, the freer and more flexible it becomes. A mind completely *connected* would certainly be, at this extreme, a mind infinitely *free*. . . ." Such an intelligence is, moreover, pure and absolute. Authentic purity is the purity of the sea, into whose imperturbable immensity all rivers flow, not of the white sepulchers beyond the shore. The dead in "Le Cimetière marin" are like *idées fixes*: their seeming absolutism is mere rigidity, which time can crumble—"To an impervious nothingness they're thinned." The authentic absolute is not something rigid and clutched; but like the rhythmic immobility of the sea and its quiet roof of sky, or like the "floating cincture" in "La Ceinture," it "sets trembling in the breath of air the ultimate tie between one's silence and the world."

PHILIP WHEELWRIGHT

IDÉE FIXE

A Duologue by the Sea

For Professor Henri Mondor
and all my friends in
the medical profession

To The Reader

THIS BOOK is the child of haste. It should be taken for what it is: an occasional work, improvised from start to finish. Though it was intended for a highly critical audience—the medical profession—it had to be done quickly, thus taking on all that hurried work involves in the way of risks, rashness, and impurities. When the mind is pressed for time, that outer compulsion prevents it from applying those within. Its own ideal standards are put aside: it relaxes its rigor, finds the quickest way out, by way of its least resistances, and relies for results on its own chance responses.

But this is just what happens in familiar talk. Between people who know each other well enough to avoid any misunderstanding as to how much is serious, how much not so serious, in what they say, everything comes down to a lighthearted game of give and take. Like the painted kings on playing cards, the most solemn subjects can be tossed on the board, along with any and every trifle the world and the moment happen to offer. . . .

The same applies in this instance. What is offered for the reader's consideration is not the "ideas" which our two men by the sea happen to be exchanging, but the exchange in itself: the "ideas" are simply the pieces in a game where rapidity is the essential thing. Our two men are wasting their time at a great rate: what they say amounts only to the elementary forms of what they could say, and such terms as "Implex" and "Omnivalence" are not to be taken for more than a kind of harmless amusement. True, most of the terms actually current in Psychology are hardly more "convenient" or precise than these.

As to the form, since the Author was hard pressed (as already pointed out) and had to make quick work of it, he decided to match the disarray of a mind under pressure with the random to-and-fro, the natural disorder of a free and easy conversation; so he had to "write as one talks"—good advice perhaps, in the days when people knew how to talk.

En roscas de cristal serpiente breve.
DON LUIS DE GÓNGORA

I WAS prey to real torments: certain very acute, very active preoccupations were destroying the rest of my world and my mind. Any distraction that might occur simply threw me back the more desperately into my plight. Added to this was the bitterness and humiliation of being bested by things of the mind—things, after all, that are made for oblivion. The kind of disturbance that has a thought for its apparent cause keeps that thought in being, and hence renews, prolongs, and reinforces itself. More than that: it *perfects* itself in a way: grows ever more subtle, cunning, powerful, resourceful, and impregnable. A thought that can torture a man escapes the conditions of thought: it becomes *another*, a parasite.

However much I tried to regain my mental equanimity, and reduce what were only ideas to the state of ideas pure and simple, it meant only an instant of effort followed by deeper anguish. It was useless reminding myself that worry, anger, this enormous weight on the chest, this grappled feeling round the heart, were no justifiable consequences of a few mental images. "Someone else," I would tell myself, "if he could see them in my mind, would remain quite unmoved. . . ." Or, "In three years' time," I would say, "these very phantoms will have lost all their power. . . ." And I would feel an insane longing to achieve mentally in a few moments what it would take two or three years to do. But how can we manufacture time?

And how destroy the *absurd*—the very thing we indulge and encourage when we delight in it?

I cannot say what saved me from desperate remedies. . . . I kept to the simplest: work and movement. Violently, capriciously, I treated my body and mind like a tyrant. I set them difficult tasks: on a small scale I did what humanity does by its researches; digging deeper so as not to see. But I would quickly tire of my self-imposed trials. Their indirect purpose would suddenly ruin their immediate one. There was no way of cheating my appetite for pain and worry: the substitution would not work.

I began a series of day-long wanderings, making the town and sea front my beat. But mere walking on a level only stimulates the action of thought, which can hurry the pace or slow it down, but is in no way hindered by it. A steady pace will lend itself to any kind of madness, being equally the slave of our demons or our gods. In earlier years I had known the pace prompted by happy invention, the exhilaration of a body driven gaily on by the impulse of song and its divine birth. Now I was driven in flight from my own thoughts. Here, there, and everywhere I carried this killing burden of irritation, fury, tenderness, and impotence. Something dreaming in my hands would make them grasp and twist, unconsciously shaping forms and acts; and then I would find them clenched and murderous. And every moment I was in some other place than where I was: and in place of whatever I might be looking at, I would see every possible cause for lamenting.

What could be more resourceful than an incarnate and virulent obsession whose poisonous sting drives life on, against and beyond itself? Ceaselessly it retouches and revives all the inexhaustible scenes and crises of hope and despair, with an ever-growing precision far surpassing the *finite* precision of any reality.

I would walk and walk; well aware that being driven on by the exasperated mind in no way deterred the atrocious insect whose sting in my spiritual body kept up a scalding pain inseparable from my very existence. This inner burning destroyed the values of the visible world. Neither the sun, nor the earth reflecting its glitter, seemed able to dazzle me. Objects simply thwarted and irritated my obsessions; and passers-by were less noticeable than their shadows on the road. I could concentrate on nothing but earth or sky.

This particular road led seawards. A lighthouse lantern glittered above the foliage.

An immense clear screen of the tenderest color stretched bare and smooth to eye level, beyond the pliant golden masses of the trees that rocked in the offshore wind; and someone inside me called me a fool and madman.

At once I could feel the force, and the vanity of the force, that kept me from enjoying this calm magnificence, from being a part of the present moment. I drew to a halt, and hesitated, as if between . . . appearances and phantom imaginings, reality and life.

Then it occurred to me that the only thing is to break the vicious circle of imaginary ills and the rhythm of their attacks. An anguish of mental origin, created by a whole complex of contributory causes, should be countered by recourse to some strong and basic instinct.

This was why, after a feverish rush to the shore, where all was broken rocks of every size and every possible shape, I set myself the laborious task of picking my way among the *total* disorder of their shattered forms and weirdly precarious angles. Here was a way of forcing that amazing machine, the human body, to produce at each moment a new and particular adjustment that demanded the utmost concentration of its powers of foresight and adaptation, and its most contradictory faculties.

Involved as I was in leaps and clamberings, with all the difficulties of a rigorously broken-up surface, beset with every obstacle and cleft with always unforeseen little canyons, at the same time I could feel, on the alert inside me, that black point from which, at the slightest respite, the fever of inner convulsions, of intolerable arguments for and against, would once again break loose. The absurd was still lying in wait for me. I chose the riskiest paths among the rocks. As if my plague might lose track of me! Reason and presence of mind were here at a natural advantage. For my own safety I had to act without error or delay, on pain of injuring myself. In this chaos of stone there was never a step or a concerted movement that resembled another or could serve my purpose twice.

The sea kept vanishing and reappearing before my eyes. I could hear it contentedly lapping, very softly, and then beginning again: beating out its measure of infinite time.

Drawing nearer I found, below the rocks, heaped-up masses of the concrete blocks that protect the outworks of a seaport.

I began jumping from one cube to another, and while doing so, suddenly noticed a man, down there between two of these gigantic dice.

A line led out from him to the water. A basket and a small painter's outfit lay in his shadow.

I was feeling in anything but a *humane* frame of mind. To someone running away from himself, worn with the effort of trying to escape that self, anyone else's company is odious, since other people infallibly make us think of ourselves.

I cursed the man. Turning round before I could climb back among my rocks, he smiled. I recognized him as a doctor I had met quite a few times, with one set of friends or another.

And he recognized me from what he remembered of these encounters—and certain remarks of my own or other people's.

WELL, WELL! he said. Hello!

—Yes, it's me. . . . Are you busy painting, or fishing? Or painting and fishing?

—Not a bit of it. . . . I've got all the materials for both. But the fish needn't be very nervous. Or the landscape either. It's all just for show. . . . The fact is, my dear man, I'm doing what everybody else does on holiday, playing at something or other. Some people play at savages—or explorers. Some try to make out they're having a rest, others that they're giving themselves a real workout. . . .

—And doctors claim they've cured everybody.

—There's something in that. . . .

—And you try to make out you're painting and fishing.

—Oh, I'm not taken in. . . . The fact is, I'm trying my hand at doing nothing at all, but it's heavy going. How do you set about doing nothing? It seems to me the hardest thing in the world; worse than a labor of Hercules, it's an everlasting bugbear. You see, at the time of year when convention, propriety, custom, herd instinct—and sometimes even the temperature—insist that you clear out——

—Nobody's supposed to fall sick just then.

—Of course. . . . And—well, I *naturally* do as my colleagues do. Shut up shop. Send my patients off to spas, beaches, mountains, or the devil. And I come and roast here. . . . But on top of that, I have to do what I can to cheat my own complaint. . . .

—Your own complaint. What's that?

—The one I have.

—Something wrong with you somewhere?

—I don't know if it's somewhere. I think so, but I don't know.

—You can't localize it?

—My dear man, that's the whole trouble! Do you really want me to explain? Well, if I try to describe exactly what's the matter, I can only say I've got something wrong with . . . my time! . . .

—You don't mean it! . . .

—Yes sir, I do. To put it more explicitly: I've got the *disease of activity*. I can't, I don't know how to do nothing . . . how to stay two minutes without ideas, without words, without doing something useful! . . . So, off I go to some deserted nook, with my paraphernalia—the insignia of an empty mind. Their whole function is to make you keep still, force you into long sedentary spells of—emptiness.

—In fact you're trying to carry out what the Pre-Raphaelites called "An Entire Adherence to the Simplicity of Nature"?

—Every now and then I gaze at my empty creel, my naked canvas, and I try to urge my brain to do likewise. . . . And how about you?

—Me? . . . Leave *me* out of it. . . . But this disease of activity sounds interesting. You seriously think it's a disease?

—I assure you, said the Doctor. I'm in real pain.

—In pain?

—I mean I *ought* to be. . . .

—In the words of Berenice to Titus, I might say: You are a physician, Doctor, and in pain!

—My friend, a doctor feels it more than most.

—*Similia similibus.* . . . You cap my verse with doggerel.

—We know better how to feel pain. And so we feel it more. There's a very close link between pain and understanding. . . . And then, we know our own limitations all too well.

—But haven't you a whole arsenal within reach—I mean all the chemistry you're notorious for?

—Thanks, said the Doctor. That's our pact with the Devil.

(*The Doctor looked at me. I looked at the sea.*)

—Now then, I said, won't you tell me exactly what's the matter?

—I've told you: I have to be continually on the go. I've just *got* to be busy, to be functioning. . . . I can't be without some definite thing to do. Mind you, I'm anything but short of work. I'm up to the eyes in it. By evening, I feel done for. . . . But even then I can't stop. . . . I still have to go on worrying at something or other, and there are so many things to worry about nowadays. Every single day adds to, or divides up, or demolishes, what we thought we knew. . . . I sometimes wonder if the enormous accumulation of facts and hypotheses isn't simply . . . our way of reacting to an increasing excitation of the mind. Do you follow?

—Yet another hypothesis, eh?

—Naturally.

—You mean, the more we find the more we seek, and the more we seek the more we find?

—That's right. I sometimes think the same relationship has grown up between research and discovery as between the drug and the addict.

—Odd. And so the whole transformation of the modern world . . .

—Is a result. In fact, is simply another aspect of it. Cult of speed. Abuse of the senses. . . . The need for excessive lighting, incoherent sensations, movement. The itch for the bigger and bigger . . . the mindless drive towards the more and more "advanced" thing in politics, in art—and . . . even in morals.

—And you feel the same addiction in yourself?

—I know all too well how everything keeps multiplying and dividing itself up in my brain. At every other moment, willy-nilly, some idea, observation, or analogy becomes an insistent presence—a sort of mental thorn. . . .

—Doctor, your brain's nothing but a culture-broth swarming with question marks! . . .

—And do you know how I arrived at a definition of my peculiar complaint?

—No.

—I can reduce it to a very simple formula: fatigue stimulates me. The more tired I am, the more I want to do. That is the capital symptom. Obviously, this is where the abnormal comes in.

—But I know that symptom of old. A friend of mine must have noticed the same thing in me. Sometimes, if we were talking and I was beginning to monopolize the conversation, he would take me by the arm and look at me and say, "You're talking too well this evening, old man. You must be very, very tired. . . ." And he was never wrong.

—What a keen eye he had. . . .

—True enough. . . . And that very instant I would feel dead tired. Although I hadn't noticed until then.

—There's nothing to prove that a man who *ought* to feel very tired always does feel very tired.

—And what about your own case? Can't you do anything for it? Go and see a colleague, a neurologist, a . . . psychiatrist!

—Are you joking?

—Good Lord, surely anything that might foil your inner enemy, blunt that thorn in your mind. . . . After all, it's some kind of obsession. . . .

—Not at all, far from it! . . . I'm not a monomaniac. . . . I don't have an *idée fixe*! . . .

—But who's talking about an *idée fixe*? I abominate that expression. Don't you agree it's a very clumsy term?

—You could say *Mono-ideism.*

—It would be a public calamity.

—Well. . . . One more wouldn't matter. . . . Anyhow, the thing exists.

—It does not.

—How do you mean?

—There's no such thing as an *idée fixe*. What is really meant is something quite different, that needs a different name. I tell you, *idée fixe* is a very clumsy term.

—What does it matter? The thing exists. And you know that quite as well as I do. There's a fixation and an intensity of ideas that amounts to the pathological. That's a fact. Nothing could be surer, could it? And I think the term fits perfectly.

—It's absolutely misconceived. And I'll tell you why.

—Go on! . . . But you're right in the middle of an *idée fixe* yourself, my dear man!

—I say I'll tell you why.

—Very well. Why?

—It's simply that an *idea* can't be *fixed*. There you are. That's all.

—It's not much. In that case, what do you make of all the dementias, quasi-dementias, persecution manias, the cranks and the visionaries who are diagnosed, typed, and . . . put away by us doctors every day? . . . Then again, those are just the extreme cases, the dangerous and certifiable ones. . . . And there are still plenty of other *fixed ideas* around, on the streets and—even on the rocks!

—You mean trite and trotabout ideas! . . .

—Now be serious. Of course . . . you're right in a way: there's nothing like an *idée fixe* for trotting about. . . . And I wonder just what *you* were doing, hopping up and down there, among the rocks? . . .

—Perhaps I was doing *away* with an *idée fixe.*

—You certainly looked like it.

—Well, do you want to listen to my refutation or not?

—Go ahead. . . . Expound your theory.

—But it's no such thing! I'm not inventing anything. I am simply pointing out what anybody can see for himself. It's simply that an idea cannot be *fixed.* Fixity applies (if to anything) then only to what is *not* an idea. An idea is a modification—or rather, one kind of modification—and it may even be the most intermittent kind. . . . Look. Clear your mind of theory, and just you try to *fix* an idea. . . . I'll time you. . . . But it's no good! An idea is a means, or a *transformation sign*, which more or less affects the system as a whole. But nothing stands still in the mind. I defy you to make it do so. Everything in the mind is transitional . . . though almost everything in it is renewable.

—Transformation, you say? What of, exactly?

—Ah, there you've got me. . . . Wait a moment.

—I'm waiting.

—Wait until I've hit on it. . . . I mean until I've reached a certain point. . . .

—A "threshold"? You've rung the bell and you're standing waiting!

—Yes: for a certain moment of transformation. My hesitation at this point will become an answering . . . illumination—an event. . . . A certain . . . tension will transform itself into an act. Into a word, a phrase . . .

—And you tell me you don't theorize! . . .

—Look, Doctor, suppose your mind is very preoccupied—with some worry, serious business, a big decision to be taken, some painful memory you can't get rid of, some lurking doubt. . . .

—Thanks. You needn't go on.

—Good. Now, what is happening in your mind?

—In my mind? What's happening is simply that I'm nursing an *idée fixe*. . . .

—Nothing of the sort. . . . What's happening is that this dominating idea takes on a peculiar value—which is not a fixity. Anything but! . . . On the contrary, I say that it *assumes* (note that term) a series of altogether novel and different properties. First, it acquires—or is given—the power of recurring *more often than it ought to*. . . .

—Elementary.

—No, this is all-important. To put it more scientifically, you might say that the probability of its conscious recurrence is modified—increased—until it becomes excessive. Your *idée fixe* is simply one that is singled out—a marked card—a number that comes up nine times out of ten on the roulette wheel. . . .

—So if I'm worried, you say it's because I'm a roulette wheel! . . . My friend, it's about time I had you locked up! . . .

—One moment, executioner. . . . I was saying that this idea tends to steal the turn of the others, meaning that anything can prompt its recurrence. Any excuse will do to bring it on stage.

—It's the star performer. . . .

—Yes, always taking the lead. It upstages the others automatically. Anything that happens can recall it. Any excuse will serve to bring it on again with all its retinue. . . . The whole routine works as if all other events—sensations, ideas, etc.—were mere distractions, interruptions. . . .

—Of what?

—Of this transitive state which seems to me to be the characteristic condition of the mind.

—You think the mind's a sort of fly that flutters here and there . . . alighting, taking off. . . .

—Yes. Not quite. But the instability, the discontinuity, the irregular flight of the fly might well represent . . .

—The mind of an idiot.

—The normal condition of our own. *Normal* isn't quite the word. The state of . . . *nonattention* which is obviously more common than any other.

—It's not so easy to define.

—Not impossible, though. It's a state where anything can replace anything else. If the life of the mind could be recorded as a continuity, it would be a revelation of . . . *total* disorder and incoherence. Now if you will allow me to overdraw my account a little . . .

—A small draft, with no guarantees, mind you.

—I would say that in this condition the images or notions that follow each other have only a purely . . . *linear* connection between them. . . . Their relationship with each other is that of mutual succession and substitution. But if a more complex relationship begins to establish itself between them, then a change must arise . . . and we move over into the world of *attention.*

—You're none too clear.

—Let's see now. . . . To think of . . . any particular thing is surely to specialize some . . . faculty, function, system, whatever you may call it . . . which is capable of thinking of —a particular thing? And does that not mean restricting something which is in itself more *generalized* than any particular object of thought—something which can be free between one engagement and another . . .

—Like the tenor at the Casino.

—Like the eye—between two points of focus.

—Ah, now I begin to see.

—Well then, my belief, or feeling, or idea is that this system or faculty has an invincible tendency to regain its own freedom. . . .

—Oh, oh! . . .

—Its own freedom—the freedom to produce, or to submit to, *something else. Something else* is the rule, the norm. . . . And this "something else," this expression of a demand for change by the life of the mind constitutes . . . the *idea.* The nature of an idea is to *intervene.* . . .

—For pity's sake! . . .

—Yes. I mean "idea" in a functional sense—the idea as event—as manifestation of the basic and systematic instability of our . . . mental existence. Look: consider yourself! . . . Can you fix an idea? You can only think in terms of modifications. If an idea, as such, remained a constant, it would no longer be an "idea."

—Then what would it be?

—Heavens, I don't know. It's hard to conceive. It would become an object . . . a pain, perhaps? . . . And even then, the most constant pain varies in intensity, in its pressure upon consciousness. . . . Conversely, any thought which lasts longer than it should becomes a *feeling* . . . makes itself felt as . . . a *deviation.* But from what? It becomes painful—a physical sensation. You might say a resistance had arisen which transformed into a fact of the sensible order something which was prevented from following its course in the realm . . . of ideas. . . . So you have a feeling of constriction which disfigures, confuses, and soon consumes your thought—just as the fixity of the eye, the continual staring at a given point, makes that point disappear and so disfigures perception. Continued fixity is impossible.

—The same, said the Doctor, as in the case of static muscular tension; to hold even a slight weight with the arm outstretched can last only a moment.

—Exactly. It is infinitely harder to remain fixed than to use up one's effort in moving about. Stillness is the unattainable value. The human body might be said to abhor prolonged specialization. It pulls us back with a jerk to the condition of free availability. . . . For instance, I find it positively painful to watch a ballerina, mounted up on one toe. . . .

—There's a specialist for you! . . . I can picture the girl's entire muscular system, starting from the big toe that carries the whole body.

—What a splendid anatomico-physiological construction she would make. . . . Leonardo would have enjoyed visualizing and drawing that ballerina flayed, suspended in a state of triply unstable equilibrium!

—Why triply?

—Obviously . . . from a muscular, nervous, and mechanical point of view. Three good reasons for losing it.

—And then off she runs to make love. . . .

—There you are again. . . . Instability. . . .

—Making love?

—Can last only a moment. . . . Otherwise you'd die of it. What could be nearer to pain?

—Exquisite pain, said the Doctor. There's an excellent example of your theory of distraction and the brevity of all concentration.

—Thanks. . . . I hadn't thought of it. It's most significant. But the phenomenon of love has something . . . blinding about it, which makes it impossible to think about, except in terms of a moralist . . . or an immoralist: I mean, to other people's cost . . . or one's own advantage.

—The fact is that it's hard to consider it coolly. . . .

—You think so? . . . It seems that many people can even reason about it. . . . For instance, a while ago I read a certain remark that seems to me very true: "There is clearly one cause for a declining population: presence of mind. A race of married couples who are mindful of the future constitutes a nation that is careless of its future. Either they must put an end to their caution or to the race."

—That's amusing. . . . Who wrote it?

—A not very readable writer. . . . I forget his name. A Hermetic. . . .

—He seems clear enough this time. He must have forgotten to cover up. Anyhow, it's a true enough remark. Races will come to an end (among other causes) through the antagonism between self-consciousness and procreation; . . . between life and thought; between calculation and . . . inspiration.

—The lady should have married a dancer; and instead she fell to a computer! . . . And to think that jurists declare: *To give and to withhold is not . . .*

—But there's man for you! . . . Fundamentally, he only escapes animality by certain inhibitions which are more subtle, more rarefied, than those of the animals. He holds back, picks and chooses, for and against.

—Queer animal! . . . Capable at once of minute reasoning, sustained attention, doubts and reservations—and on the other hand, a creature of impulse, a slave to his reflex actions. . . . At one moment a machine for thinking, clarifying, suspending judgment—a machine for eluding the mechanical. And then an hour later . . .

—There's a cerebrospinal short-circuit.

—Exactly. The fuses blow. I wonder if the electric eel, after paralyzing his prey, doesn't feel a similar reaction.

—He's never been a patient of mine.

—Don't you think, Doctor, that that very particular sensation, that overwhelming, conclusive . . .

—And rather well-known sensation . . .

—That hyperacute instant, that uttermost . . .

—Call it a shock.

—Yes, that climax, in fact, is a limit, a *nec plus ultra* . . .

—You're overdoing it.

—It isn't possible to overestimate the force behind the idea and the memory of that supreme moment. . . .

—Supreme? Why *supreme*?

—Because it puts such an abrupt finish to something. . . . What I meant is that that fraction of a second plays a tremendous part in every man's life history. . . .

—Nothing precisely new in all this, my dear fellow!

—Oh, new or old, what does it matter in the case of ideas! Now, don't you think it's surprising to note that history (which is the sum total of the life histories of mankind) leaves no room for this . . . obsession? *A good supper, a good bed,* and . . . *this other thing* we are talking about: it seems to me these are the three axes of all history. . . .

—But don't you see, history doesn't bother about men as such. History in the books, history as taught, is almost entirely concerned with official events. It's above all a picture album; and sometimes a lot of guesswork based on abstractions. . . . Look: it's only a short while since people realized that navigation on the grand scale dates from the Thirteenth Century. Why? Because before that there was neither compass nor rudder. The idea of fixing a hinged flap to an axle on the poop, movable by a tiller, is a late invention. It allows for expansion and manipulation of sails; with better maneuvering, more can be attempted: men can brave the Atlantic, discover America, and . . . since we were talking of sex . . .

—It suffered a good deal from the invention of the rudder.

—Yes, you see at once where it leads, said the Doctor. From America comes a small pale personage . . .

—Whose descendants have multiplied amazingly over here. It seems as if we all have him on our minds, more or less; and but for him, quite a number of remarkable things would never have been dreamed of, even . . .

—How right you are, said the Doctor. The introduction of syphilis into Europe is certainly a more important event than the Treaty of Utrecht.

—I'm afraid so!

—And it's never mentioned. . . . The landing of the treponemata in Europe has been of far graver importance to humanity than all the plenipotentiaries in the world. . . . And do you know that the stegomyia completely wiped out a whole civilization in Mexico?

—Everything depends on the criterion of importance you choose. . . . But to come back to sex. . . .

—Sex, said the Doctor, is a weird mechanism. You struggle like . . . a dog to attain . . . a threshold . . .

—An ecstasy! . . . A lightning flash. . . . But then, everything of value in life is essentially brief.

—Essentially?

—*Essentially*. That's the point, the nub, the crux. There's food for thought in that essential brevity. . . . *Intensity, brevity, rarity*.

—*Equality, Fraternity*, and so forth, said the Doctor. I can't see what you are trying to get at.

—Neither can I. I'm pulling at a single thread of the skein in my head. Sometimes its the *sense*, sometimes it's the *sound* that . . .

—You poor man. . . .

—It's a trick of my trade. You know, of course, that the absurd is the material I work in. So don't be surprised at the leaps I take, in the form of preposterous questions . . . or rather wild pronouncements. . . . For instance, I was just about to say something appalling.

—I can take it, said the Doctor.

—We were talking of sex—the physiology of love.

—Which is what it is, said the Doctor.

—You said it amounted to a tremendous struggle to attain a threshold. . . .

—Of course. . . . Fundamentally, it's like a . . . sneeze!

—Well, who knows whether the Universe . . .

—Oh! Oh! . . .

—Agreeing, of course, that the word has a meaning that will . . . withstand inspection.

—Why not?

—Or at least that we can qualify the word, make it fit into a proposition. . . .

—Why not, why not?

—But how do you suppose that the All can be conveyed by any possible image or idea? The All can have no recognizable form.

—You think not?

—No. . . . Anyway, that doesn't matter at all . . . for the moment.

—To my mind, said the Doctor, the Universe must be something like fireworks on a Fourteenth of July night . . . or else a cloud—like the cloud formed by a spoonful of dye or spirit dropped into a glass of water.

—In any case, I said, what I meant was that the Universe can just as well be considered as . . . a gigantic *struggle*, a gigantic process of transformation. . . .

—Gigantic being a feeble term, rejoined the Doctor. . . . And so you think that . . . it's *meant* to arrive at something?

—A man cannot conceive of anything that is not . . . directed, that does not *tend to* or *towards*. . . . The nature of our actions in general imposes itself on our thought, weighs on our expressions. . . .

—*For example*, said the Doctor, one of our most vital actions, that of eating and digesting. Generally speaking, we're a one-way tube! . . .

—And that is one of the origins of our grotesque idea of time. . . . The *future*: appetence, salivation, excitation of one gland after another. . . . The *present*: tasting, chewing, digestion, assimilation. . . .

—As for the *past*, said the Doctor, you needn't go into that; let's get back to the Universe.

—Well, this Universe in labor has perhaps only one purpose—or secret incentive—the quest for *consciousness*—and thence—for a certain *thought* . . . the Supreme Thought.

—Its *idée fixe*?

—The *threshold* of the existence of the All.

—I don't know, said the Doctor. And neither do you. There's a lot of anthropomorphism in what you say.

—And what the devil else do you expect? Anthropos can

only practice anthropomorphism. And anthropopsychism. There's no way out of it.

—Look here, said the Doctor, there are certain cases nevertheless where we can exclude anthropomorphism and all its train—determinism, and so on.

—I'd be only too glad to believe it. . . . But——

—Well, said the Doctor. . . . If I say, "I have five fingers on my hand." . . . Where can you find the anthropomorphism in that?

—It's obvious. . . . Only the gross vision of man, and his clumsy common sense, would evolve a makeshift like: *One and one are two.* For a more subtle being, there would no doubt be neither concrete units nor things that could be sufficiently confused or assimilated as to be sorted into groups. . . . Every "concept"—as it is called—is a makeshift.

—What a sophist! . . . But whether it's anthropomorphism or not, it seems to me the proposition that the world is a tendency to thought is invalid, hopeless. . . . It means giving thought a sort of absolute price or value.

—I'm far from wanting to do that, I must say.

—Lord yes. . . . You won't even tolerate an *idée fixe.*

—Certainly not. . . . I've already given you my reasons . . . I allow for ideas that are . . . favored . . . above the normal . . . for ideas . . . characterized by abnormal frequency, for ideas so easily stimulated that all other ideas, all sensations and events—everything *else*, in fact—become, to a degree, errors, infringements. . . .

—Of what?

—Of what. . . . Wait. . . . I haven't found that out yet. . . .

—We've all the time in the world. The air's so clear, the sea's so . . . wide. I light a cigarette. I'm enjoying the first puff, while you're busy worrying your scalp. Speech is silver, silence is golden.

—Got it! No . . . that isn't quite it! Well, let's say provisionally that . . . this obsessive—but not fixed—idea is . . . how shall I put it? . . . is . . . if you'll forgive the word . . . *omnivalent*. . . . It attaches to everything. . . . Or: everything attaches to it. . . .

—*OMNIVALENT!* . . . Splendid! *Omnivalent* is . . . sublime! "On Omnivalent Ideas." "On the Omnivalence of Ideas." "On Omnivalence as a Depressive Stimulus." What a discovery! . . . I can see all the articles on it. . . . What a title! . . . What an appetizer! "On Omnivalence, and the Treatment of Abnormal Favorites." . . . "On Omnivalent, Anti-logical Hyperfavoritism." My dear man, you must let me have that word, and I'll launch its career. . . . From this moment I renounce the . . . nonpursuit of art, and the nonpractice of fishing, and I'll set about an article for *Brain*—something really remarkable, something that will hit the bull's-eye! . . . What a piece—with a title like that! Don't you see, my dear fellow, your *Omnivalence* will soon take its place in the Dictionary of the Academy . . .

—Of Medicine?

—Naturally!

—And what will the article be about?

—About you, of course. . . .

—Good Lord! . . .

—Please continue! *Omnivalent* is a godsend. . . .

—All right. I'll go on.

—You're on top of your form. *Omnivalent* is a pearl of real price.

—Thanks. A pearl implies a mollusk.

—Well . . . mollusks are not classed among the more excitable types. They're creatures of habit—of an *idée fixe*. We're still right inside our subject.

—Doctor, you're doing nothing but make game of me.

—Far from it, my friend. . . . I'll put it this way: the weather's glorious, we are chatting away—and I can think of nothing more delectable, more . . . titillating than what we're doing, trifling to and fro on the surface of . . .

—What?

—Everything. Our minds. Our problems . . .

—Our worries. Our cares. Our . . . life history.

—To bob about and swim in what we don't know, with the help of what little we do! It's heavenly!

—Man was made for conversation. I believe that in all seriousness.

—So you think cafés were foreordained in the plan of the Cosmos?

—I wasn't shown the plan. Haven't been consulted. But don't forget, the Revolution was a product of the cafés.

—Another oversight on the part of History.

—Anyhow, it's certainly an enormous gap in Literary History. The whole of French Literature, from the seventeenth century to our day, was fashioned, fomented, controlled by the salons and the cafés. But that's all over now. . . .

—A pity.

—There it is. . . . Like you, everyone's got something wrong with his time nowadays.

—No more conversation?

—It's scarce—and poor.

—Well, to compensate, I hope we're growing more . . . profound?

—It doesn't seem so to me. And anyway—*profound*? I strongly suspect there are some gross delusions behind the efforts we make to dig into ourselves. . . . Some people think they can dig down to the earliest strata of their lives. . . . As a rule, they're only in search of obscene fossils.

—They wouldn't search if they hadn't already found.

—True enough. And others imagine that this is a way of getting in touch with . . . their *real* selves, in return for a bit of inner concentration and a sort of . . . suppression of things outside, achieved with the greatest difficulty. . . . They don't realize that they are only inflicting a peculiar distortion on themselves. . . . They are striving to adjust their sensitive consciences to some inconceivable reverted vision—to something *within*. . . . In short, there may be depths that are *accessible* (but what's to be found there is hardly worth diving down for) and others that are *unfathomable*. . . . Even if we could venture that deep and see anything, there would be no means of understanding what we found.

—For my own part, I'm a fundamentalist. If I look into myself, I find . . . there are things one can tell other people, and other things one can only tell oneself. . . . And still others that one can't even admit to oneself. . . . There's a certain amount of dirt there, obviously. And since it's common to all, not much interest attaches to it. But besides all that there are things that loom . . . powerful, indistinct. . . .

—Yes, indeed. Things that have no likeness to anything. . . . This is where we peer into the life of the viscera.

—Stop! No entry. Death to intruders. . . . Let's keep to the surface. . . . And talking of surfaces, is it true that you once said or wrote: *Nothing is deeper in man than his skin*?

—True.

—What did you mean by it?

—Couldn't be simpler. . . . One day, feeling tired to death of the words "profound" and "profundity" . . .

—Which we've just been bandying about ad lib. . . . Look, I diagnose in you a morbid sensitivity about words. You're shying and rearing at them every minute! Hang it all, they're just a makeshift! . . . Life has no time for this hair-splitting. We've got to work out what we can. Napoleon said you make war by engaging the enemy on all fronts and then seeing what happens. . . .

—He said anything you like about war, from every angle. . . . Besides, people who've really practiced a thing, when they try to express or convey their experience—it's a universal rule—they offer the most contradictory precepts. . . . You'll find that even in the Gospels. . . .

—And even in medicine, I must say. . . .

—Yes. Even Hippocrates. . . . Just you try to combine *principiis obsta* with *quieta non movere*. . . .

—We do our best. But let's come back to you. You're jibbing at every word. . . . There's no peace, talking to you. Every minute there's an upset. You've reached the stage when you can't even talk to yourself. How the dickens can you expect, in such conditions, to formulate a single idea? That's what I wonder.

—My dear Doctor, I prefer to be fully conscious of getting nowhere—rather than do the same thing . . . unawares. . . . Well then, I was annoyed, I was feeling exasperated with *profound* and *profundity*. . . .

—I bet you'd been reading some article on Pascal.

—I won't take your bet. Any more than I'll take Pascal's. . . .

—All right. So then?

—Then? . . . I remembered what the medical books say about the development of the embryo. One fine day, it creates a fold, a crease in its outer envelope. . . .

—The ectoderm. And it closes up. . . .

—Alas, yes! . . . And all our troubles start from there! . . . *Chorda dorsalis*! And then marrow, brain, everything needed to make us feel, suffer, think . . . and be *profound*. That's where it all starts. . . .

—So what?

—Well, the whole process is invented by the *skin*! . . .

However much we dig, Doctor, we remain . . . ectodermal.

—Yes, but . . . there are extensions.

—We can penetrate as far as the viscera. . . . But there we have no highly perfected instruments. Nothing to compare with the complex mechanisms, the sensory arrangement, to be found in the eye and ear. Way inside there, everything's coarse, brutish. It can hardly say more than "good" or "bad."

—Generally, "bad."

—And yet there's nothing more potent, is there? . . . There are mighty despots in there who act without any explanation. . . . Life would be bearable if it weren't for the viscera!

—You want to reduce me to beggary?

—In short, the life of the senses exerts a very unequal pressure, its means are very unlike, according to whether it expands towards the surface or plunges into the masses. . . .

—The laboring masses. I feel certain you have a fitful digestion. And our liver is slightly enlarged. . . .

—I don't doubt it. And that's why I round off my theorem like this: Nothing is deeper in man than his skin—*in so far as he knows himself.* But *in so far as he does not know himself*, nothing is deeper in man than his liver and . . . suchlike things . . . whether neutral or . . . helpful.

—What a piece of neutromania! You certainly work up some dubious connections! . . .

—Well, how's this for a nervous-liverish connection! How do you account for the fact that, one fine morning, on receiving a really . . . shattering letter—but one that called for some concentration in order to gather its full import—the moment that letter was opened and glanced at rather than read, I had the atrocious feeling of a knife stuck into my *liver*?

—There's no explanation. Of course, we could cover it with a formula that might satisfy and soothe, for the time being. . . .

—And how do you explain that an idea, an object of painful reflection that happens for the moment to be completely dismissed, disguised, concealed from the mind by some other subject that seems to take up all one's thoughts, should be abruptly, brutally recalled, not by "association of ideas"—so called—but by a sudden twinge near the heart?

—We're down in the depths again. . . .

—Wait. We were quibbling about the *idée fixe* a minute ago.

—And we aren't finished, I suspect.

—I objected . . .

—I grant you that.

—Now let me just comment on another, even commoner expression.

—I can see you're in form. You must be awfully tired.

—Never mind. What about you?

—Me? . . . Oh, I'm listening.

—Well, I may be full of objections, but . . . take an expression like "a dreary idea" . . . it's common enough, commoner than *idée fixe*. Or the expression, "a gloomy notion."

—So now you're going to abolish the whole idea of gloomy ideas! Cure all the melancholiacs in one fell swoop? . . .

—No, unfortunately. All I maintain is that an *idea* can't be *dreary*. The same idea that overwhelms poor Tom leaves Dick quite unmoved. As for Dick's potentialities for melancholy, they'll find their own source, or excuse, or appearance. . . .

—I think all this is a bit farfetched. . . .

—It's no novelty. . . .

—It's too plausible.

—The ancients had an inkling of these things. The four temperaments. . . .

—Oh, the ancients! . . .

—They fumbled about just as we do. They fumbled about in direct experience, just as we do in the field of the microscope.

—It's a devilishly fertile field, that.

—Yes. But I have the impression that it's enormously more prolific in problems than solutions. Such, it seems, is the fate of research when its medium is a different order of magnitude. The researcher starts out with hopes that are . . . curiously contradictory . . .

—Contradictory?

—Of course. . . . He hopes to make new discoveries.

—Naturally.

—And he does. But he wants the new discoveries to be sufficiently like what we've found out already to be easily understandable. And that isn't always the case. . . . Far from it. The more we advance into the minute, the less we *understand.* Some physicists have pushed so far into microscopic analysis that they've got lost in a world where Old Causality no longer applies. . . . For what's to be done in an order of magnitude where there are no more images? . . . If things have an *ultimate nature,* that nature has no resemblance to anything. . . . *Resemblance no longer exists.* . . . The ultimate is meaningless. How very strange it is, this search, via the minutest possible analysis, for the key to the problems of our order of being! . . .

—Which doesn't alter the fact that the microscope has tremendous uses. . . .

—I'm talking as a layman.

—You seem to me to take a passionate interest in everything that isn't your own business.

—What do you expect? I'm a *Man.* Which means I have to do what is useless. Have you ever studied animals, Doctor?

—Not nearly as much as our own species.

—I've often considered them. And do you know what I think I've found?

—No.

—I've found . . . and this brings us straight back to your complaint—your *disease of activity*. . . . I've found—and anyhow, I've noticed the same thing with children. . . . Children, my dear Doctor, certainly don't suffer from *that* complaint.

—What on earth do you mean? . . . What children can you be talking about? If they're fit and well, all children are absolute *monsters* of activity. Just you try to make them sit still . . . the little devils! . . . If they see a tap, they've got to turn it; a bell, and they have to pull it. Failing that, they'll have a pull at their own tongues! They'll meddle with, fiddle with, maneuver anything that seems to work, right way or wrong. They'll play the devil if they can with everything in reach: but above all, with their own four limbs—not to mention the faces they'll pull and the howls they'll give. . . . And the same with any hapless domestic pet that comes their way. . . . Tearing up, breaking up, building, they're always at it! And they'll cry if they can't think of anything better to do. . . . You might say they're only conscious of all the things around them in so far as they can *act* on them, or through them, in no matter what way: the action, in fact, is all. . . . Now if that isn't the plaguiest form of the disease! . . .

—No, no . . . we don't understand each other. Children's activity is quite harmless, except for parents, watches, clocks, fine books—and the thinker a floor above. But it does the doers nothing but good. You know that better than I do. And that's why I say that neither children nor animals can do anything useless. They're quite incapable of it. . . .

—Everything depends on what you call useful or useless.

—Yes, and this is where I start cheating. . . .

—I've got my eye on you.

—Very well. What I call *useless* is the action or thing for which a person feels no *immediate need.* Allow me that much; and if you do, you'll see how a child, who can give the utmost concentration to some game, will rebel against paying the slightest attention as soon as you want to make him apply himself to study. He can't see any necessity for learning to read. . . .

—I did! I cried to make people teach me!

—He has an imperious urge to get acquainted with every possible movement of his body, with his own strength, with the objects all round him. . . . He's at the growing stage. In order to grow, he has to use up . . .

—Well, speaking for myself, I played very little as a child. I was bored with games, just as I'm bored with amusements now. I mean anything qualified as such, that claims to . . .

—What about the theater?

—Never. I sleep through it.

—Films?

—They annoy me. Facts falsified.

—And what about travel?

—It tires me. The sheer compulsion of *looking*! . . . All those museums!

—Do you read?

—I can't bear novels. . . . Do you think a man who's been practicing my profession for twenty years can read fiction? . . . My whole business consists of intruding on people's lives, and intimacies, and life histories. . . .

—And . . . poetry?

—Take a good look at me!

—I see. I won't press the point. You're . . . very considerate.

—And let me add this: I can find poetry where other people don't, and I fail to find it where they do.

—That's not quite so considerate.

—I'm telling you straight what I think.

—At least you've got fishing and painting.

—As you see. . . . To put it in a nutshell, the moment I feel that a time, a place, an attitude of mind or body, indicates recreation as the order of the day—my whole being protests, yawns, flinches. . . . I start thinking about my business, my patients, my career, anything but *that*. . . .

—What a waste! Instead of giving yourself over to the useful activity of distraction, relaxation, refreshment . . . and so forth . . . you set about *fabricating the future*, which satisfies no real need; and there we have our disease of activity very well described. Did you know, Doctor, that Napoleon gave a perfect definition of it?

—Napoleon again?

—Now and again. Anyhow, he's the model of modern man—the man who no longer has time. For want of knowing how to waste it.

—Well, what did Napoleon have to say?

—He wrote it in a letter one day. He said, "I am always living two years ahead." For him, the present didn't exist.

—What a man!

—What *neurons* he had! . . . I could sum him up this way: "He could conceive the whole in relation to all its parts, and sleep whenever he chose."

—Yes, but what a terrible stomach! . . . And look at his sex life. . . .

—Yes, but what a brain! . . . Which would you rather, Doctor?

—It would be devilish hard to choose.

—Certainly. . . .

—After all, it's a question of which gives you the keener

sensation of living—the utmost awareness of . . . the *moment*, or the utmost awareness . . . of the *possible*.

—The latter is much the rarer. And the pride it brings with it is not to be sneezed at.

—Maybe. But when you've been through the asylums and seen all the emperors, popes, and millionaires in there, it rather cools off your esteem for worldly greatness—even the intellectual variety—for there are just as many poets, philosophers, inventors . . .

—But what would we do without pride?

—Get quietly on with our jobs. . . . Moreover, it can be agreed that there's a physical form of pride—I mean the euphoria that comes with the sense of having done a thing really well.

—Applause from the . . . viscera, for a brilliant comedy performed by the nerve centers, who get all the limelight. . . . In such cases, the fact is that instead of feeling tired, you feel all the stronger for the success . . . at times, lighter, more resourceful. A public speaker told me that after a speech, not a very long one, but heard with applause, he felt the urge to begin again, feeling certain he could make it even better than before. . . .

—He'd have been hissed, the second time! . . . Nothing could be more mysterious than all the interactions of organism and mind. The parts played by the physique, the constant factors in human life, by chance, circumstance, adaptation . . . all these essentially hostile conditioning forces that have to work together somehow . . . what a jungle it all adds up to. Don't forget that the mind is the domain of "values"; to *evaluate* is the grand design of the thinking system. Well, the same mental event which, on the physical plane, amounts, or ought to amount to a setback, the result of fatigue, of localized exhaustion, something "accidental," a limited response comparable to a slip of the tongue, can, on the *other* hand, take on a certain value—a literary value, for example.

—Thanks!

—Yes. It can produce a very happy, very novel effect, which the conscious mind appreciates, welcomes, collects, and notes down. . . . And then in the right context, that same little effect . . .

—Can be as good as Shakespeare!

—At least! . . .

—Ah well, Doctor, I can see that where poetry is concerned you . . . decidedly . . .

—Why can't you agree to accept the obvious?

—Because I could no longer agree to go on living.

—I've said nothing unreasonable. Nothing that you don't know as well as I do—or a hundred times better, I should say! A moment ago you were telling me yourself that the absurd was your field of operations.

—Yes, but . . .

—Did I go any further than that?

—You are making no allowance for the work involved. It seems to me that the mind tends to move from disorder to order. . . . Or, if you prefer, from a certain disorder-of-its-own to a certain order-of-its-own. In a way it works in a reverse direction to that of machinery, which transforms a unified energy into less unified. . . .

—Hmm. . . .

—Oh, it's only a crude comparison. . . . But to return to the mind: for it to carry out its characteristic labor of transformation, it has to be supplied with—*disorder*! . . .

—That's a tall order. . . .

—Why not?

—Something preposterous.

—And the mind finds its disorder where it can. In itself, outside, everywhere. . . . To function, it must have the differential *Order-Disorder*, just as a heat differential is essential to a machine, or to any phenomenon whatever! . . . But I must repeat that the comparison is . . .

—False.

—No, it isn't! . . . Yes. . . . All right then!

—And then? . . . At least you've found a justification for Poetry. . . . By sleight of hand, or in a trice. We ought to follow the fashion. *Trice* is the word they use in the papers now.

—Have you ever considered the problem of dreams, Doctor?

—Now there you've got a really fashionable phenomenon! . . . We'll soon be having a Chair of Oneiromancy at the Medical School. Though I certainly won't be the one to press for it. . . . No, thanks. . . .

—Why not?

—My dear man, I'm so fed up with the whole story and all its dirty ins and outs. . . . I've been stuffed to the skin with incestuous narcoses! . . . In fact, I've reached a point of saturation where . . . you know what I really think?

—Pronounce, O king . . .

—I begin to think there's no such thing as . . . dreams!

—Good Lord! So what happens to *Athaliah*'s dream?

—I've even dared to push myself to the point where . . . I feel convinced that dreams are . . . a dream.

—But don't you ever have any yourself?

—Lord, yes! . . . But . . . I can't legally vouch for it until . . . I'm awake. Who's to prove that it isn't a waking fabrication, a fictitious memory—a superficial and garbled account of the state of passing from absolute oblivion to conscious awareness?

—In which case, you would never be able to say, "I've

had a dream," but only, "I'm dreaming." The verb would only have meaning in the present tense. . . . And yet you can wake up sometimes, your heart pounding, in the middle of some exploit, some panic or other. . . . Could there be a more forcible proof than that?—not to mention others. . . .

—But it doesn't prove anything. A pounding heart may make us invent, on the spot, a set of pseudo-reasons for heart trouble. . . .

—That reason knoweth not.

—As usual. . . . But the invention is perhaps simply an attempt to express the fact "my heart is pounding" in the jumbled vocabulary of an organism which is passing from one state to another.

—Well, I still believe in the existence of dreams. Dreams of the good old sort.

—It's funny. Philosophers used to question whether reality wasn't a dream. Now we are doing the opposite.

—You are, anyway. But I stick to my belief in dreams; and I've a first-class reason for doing so. I gave them a great deal of thought at one time. In fact, I built up a whole . . .

—And you don't want it to be a dead loss. . . . That's understandable.

—Yes, I put a lot of speculation into the whole strange problem of dreams. In them I see the full potentialities of the . . . visceral depths making free play with the surface of mental activity: their inner turbulence finding every pretext, at every moment, for an outlet, for indirect approaches to consciousness, for expression by no matter what means. For instance, we were just talking about "gloomy notions"; well, in my view, a gloomy notion is simply a mixture of the same kind as a *dream*. . . . Gloom needs some image that will express and "explain" it. The most frightful of notions could be considered coldly, would leave us unaffected, free, if only, from another quarter—altogether *another quarter*—it were not burdened with certain . . . visceral . . . irrational values. Heart, glands, entrails—and what all—can serve as *resonators* for some image—and at times their effects are more instantaneous than the clear apprehension of that image. In fact, it might be said that, to act with greater force, their effect has to *precede* any clear and delimited view of the object—be the first to reach their strategic point of attack, whatever that may be. . . . Consider this: I have seen a small child—*infans* (not yet able to talk)—*faint away* at the sight of a little blood from a tiny cut I had given myself. How do you explain that?

—Oh, nothing's ever explained. Has anyone explained the simple fact that yawning, laughter, and nausea are all infectious?

—It's a sort of radio-communication. The transmitted image of an action travels out, and then re-forms itself as an action at a suitable point of reception. The retina serves as antenna, and something or other transforms the image into a reflex.

—Hmm. . . . What's certain is that we're a weird tissue of connections, many of which are peculiar to the individual. . . .

—They constitute our whole personality. . . .

—Some are hereditary; some, acquired—and variable, too, according to age, bodily condition, and so on. . . . My friend, we're floundering. . . .

—In fact, we know miserably little about ourselves. At most we can predict our actions a little.

—A murky business. Like meteorology!

—We have only the vaguest idea of what we're capable of. Look at all the criminals who cannot believe what they've done . . . what they would never have dreamed of doing, until the very act. . . .

—You think so?

—I do. For some, their crime was simply a sort of sudden release, after which, once all the forces of oblivion had set to work, the doer simply felt liberated. . . .

—Innocent and purer! . . .

—Well . . . purer . . . perhaps. . . .

—And if he'd come to you beforehand for advice, you'd have recommended murder?

—That's not the question. I am not offering you an apology for crime. I am trying to work out the sequence of an action. . . .

—Beware infection . . . that radio business again!

—An action that springs from the unforeseen in our personality. . . . An act in which we . . . cannot recognize ourselves . . . and for which we would gladly decline all responsibility.

—That depends. . . .

—But I agree that there's more than one person in each of us. One, for example, that only appears for a tenth of a second, or a twentieth; another that can only make its effect if it has more time at its disposal.

—In which case we would have several . . . presences. And presence of mind would simply be the prompt action whereby all their moments of consciousness would be controlled: the stops, the reservations, the withholdings, or repressive forces. I believe presence of mind consists . . . of evolving a solution based on reflection in far quicker time than the reflection itself would take.

—So it's a sort of miracle?

—Superficially. . . . In reality, we do not know how far consciousness is indispensable to one process of action or another. Certainly it ought to be, beyond a certain degree of . . . complexity. . . . Though it has its limits, varying in kind. . . . For example, I play a *trill* with these two fingers. Gently at first. . . . I am conscious of two acts, though I cannot say how I dictate them, nor how I move each finger respectively and in turn. But if I *accelerate* the trill, it's just the same as if I pressed an electric bell. A single act, on *my* part; a hailstorm of effects in the world of . . . results? . . . And note at this point (it just occurs to me) that our senses of sight and hearing correspond to certain exterior frequencies.

—I won't be a consenting party to all this, said the Doctor; you fly along like the wind, and after all, subjects like these. . . .

—Oh, I'm only skimming, of course. . . . Now if it were a question of writing . . .

—You'd be more cautious . . . you'd find something else?

—I would explore. . . .

—Aha! . . . So there's somewhere inside you . . . some limbo—some . . . cloud (I hardly know how to put it!)—where what you *might* find lies hidden, wrapped up, present yet kept in reserve, as the exact expression of what you think . . . if only you were in the mood, and had time. . . .

—And paper.

—And paper. . . .

—And the necessary stimulus. . . .

—Naturally. . . . And what next, when you have the paper in front of you?

—Ah then, I'd have to start out from what I *know* I can find, express—and isolate—*towards* that exact . . . or intense expression (which is not at all the same thing). It would be like resolving a nebula! . . .

—A nebula? . . .

—Yes. A confused mass on the confines of the moment. . . . Perhaps it would transform into a clear-cut system? Or else remain a cloudy, formless expression, an undefined intellectual adumbration. . . . But at least I can *name* that cloud, that vague luminosity. A word or two would be enough. Just as, in a day or two, or six months, simply to hear your *name*, Doctor, will recall our lovely surroundings at this moment, the outward form of our discussion, the sound of your voice. . . . And the things we are saying—the shadows of ideas that cross my mind in response to our remarks, will come back, and I will be able to rethink them, force them to become definable, to evolve, resolve themselves into precise expression. . . .

—So I'll find I've given my name to a nebula! An unexpected distinction, I must say. . . . Doctor ORION, I presume? Pleased to meet you. . . .

—Honored.

—The honor's mutual. . . . Maestro, you overwhelm me. . . . Wait till you see that article! What a debut in the Literature of Psychopathology. . . . Think of it! . . . "Omnivalence." "Intellectual Nebulae." "Crime as Catharsis." . . . And that's not all. . . .

—You'll never reach all. Meanwhile, you mix up everything I'm rash enough to try to say, and you're quite capable of cooking it all up into what you coolly describe as a *casebook*. . . .

—And what would you call it?

—I daren't tell you. . . . That particular genre—even if it is for the specialist—can be delightful to dip into. . . . I'll cut a pretty figure in *Brain*, I must say. "Edmond T. Fifty years of age. No known antecedents. Education: average. Mental age . . ." What would you give me?

—"Eleven, and three months."

—Thanks. That's just how old I feel. And what else will you put?

—"Multiparous."

—What, *multiparous*?

—Haven't you given birth any number of times?

—Who, me?

—Yes, to books.

—All dead.

—What of?

—Stillborn. . . . But what were we saying? . . . Where had we got to?

—Everywhere and nowhere. . . . If you don't mind my saying so, it's a case of losing one's bearings every minute, in your delightful company.

—Excuse me, we've got to divide the blame. You could say we're creating confusion in unison.

—Splendid. . . . "Intellectual Confusion, for solo or duet." . . . There's another famous hit! . . . A real eye-catcher. . . . I've got my article. . . .

—Then don't forget to emphasize this: that intellectual confusion, though a more or less pathological symptom in *one alone*, is normal when applied to *several*. . . . Incoherence, quibbling, *non sequiturs*, etc., are all the rule, are even indispensable in conversations, debates, discussions, in any "exchange of views," consultations, controversies . . . even in love talk, and so on. One simply wouldn't ever get anywhere, Doctor, if one understood. . . . I'll even risk saying you wouldn't understand yourself if you understood others . . . and you no longer understand others if you really understand yourself. . . . It's obvious. . . . For instance, you and I, by *the remotest of chances*, happen to meet on this rock, and in a few minutes . . .

—Pure chaos sets in!

—That's what is meant by *having a talk*, my dear Doctor.

—It's certainly refreshing. . . . Here we are: it's a superb day. Whatever remark we may make sends ripples across the surface of our cares.

—The disease of activity takes a turn for the better.

—Yes. What if we stopped talking?

—A minute's silence? . . . You be careful. . . . If we stopped talking, whatever is speaking at this moment in the air, would speak . . . in man. . . . It would perhaps say something very different. . . .

—And you don't want that?

—I think . . . maybe not.

—You cannot silence IT?

—No.

—Do you really . . . want to silence IT?

—N . . . O.

—Hey . . . that's bad . . . bad . . .

—Omnivalence.

—It's a stunningly fine day. Take a look at that billow of smoke over there, laid out on the skyline, stock-still in the perfectly still air, like a roll of dark-gray cloth. And that boat. She's been there since this morning. She's put out all she has.

—It's a tartan. They must be carrying a load of bricks.

—Anyway, it's a boat!

—No, it isn't a tartan, sorry. An old schooner . . . Italian, I dare say. . . . She could have been afloat for sixty years. The sails have been patched a thousand times. . . . But she has lovely lines, and takes the sea like a bird.

—And to think Paris exists! . . .

—Why not?

—To think that somewhere I've got . . . a telephone . . . and all the noise, and the cars, and the rain, and the hurry-scurry, and the people, and the papers! . . . And all the God Almighty fuss of all there is to do, and to think of. . . .

—Ah well, Doctor, we're not Greeks of the best period. . . .

—They didn't know their luck! . . . It seems to me they'd found out how to do while doing nothing, and how to create the finest things in the world while they sat and smoked their pipes on the sand.

—They were clever enough for that. All the same, I don't think they smoked, did they?

—True enough. But what an oversight. . . . I just can't picture all those philosophers somehow, without pipes in their mouths.

—Plato's pipe . . . but it would have been made in Tanagra, or Myrina. A marvel of grace. Can't you just see all those delightful pipes on show in a museum?

—Poor us! . . . It's strange. . . . Don't you, too, find that our daily life, seen from this distance, seems inconceivable? . . . When I think of what I have to do every day, it gives me nightmares. . . .

—And yet you never have enough of it? . . .

—Yes. But from here I can see it in proportion. . . . I can see myself . . . a little fellow, trotting here, there, everywhere, scribbling, masticating, taking his clothes off, sleeping, dressing again, running about. . . . And so on, and so on—a regular schedule. . . .

—With a few hitches. . . .

—A few hitches.

—But it's the same with everybody. . . . Isn't all this decreed, foreseen, and organized by our very being? Doesn't the heart simply spend its time beating out our time. . . .

—With a few hitches.

—And isn't our whole being rhythmically controlled or

constructed by the tempo of the workaday functions that maintain our life—just as we dispatch our routine business? . . .

—In that case . . . how is it we have any idea of anything else but our routine business? . . .

—Doctor! Don't be morbid. . . .

—And don't you start in on medical jargon.

—Sorry. Nothing's so catching as that delightful and prolific lingo. It's mocked at, or mimicked sometimes. . . . But believe me—even in Molière, even in Rabelais—there's a secret jealous admiration on the writer's part for a language where words can be coined ad lib, where a totally free invention is, in a sense, *basic* and constitutional to its system.

—Humbug! . . . Why don't you answer my question?

—I'm getting there. What I wanted to say was . . . But I've told you already. I said it seemed to me that animals could do absolutely nothing that wasn't *useful*: and by that I mean, *under some immediate external or organic pressure*. A cow can see the stars, but she deduces from that neither a Chaldean astronomy, nor a Kantian ethic, nor an everybody's homemade metaphysics. . . . She simply reduces them to zero—blots them out. It's an extraordinary thing when you look into it: perception that serves no purpose!

—You have a great big bump of wonder, my friend.

—Yes . . . I must have a resistance box somewhere in my brain. . . . Anyway, the cow takes in only such perceptions as will correspond to a uniform response, a predetermined act that is part of the life cycle of some function of her organism. The rest is null and void. If some strange object frightens her, she takes to her heels, and she'll never be tempted to come back—however cautiously—out of intellectual curiosity, to identify and classify it in her world system. . . . Her only definition of that object is flight: *something to run away from.*

—But that seems to me to be exactly our own definition of pain. . . .

—And death. . . . And that's why we don't know where to situate them in our world system. . . .

—Yes, indeed. . . . It's all very complicated. People don't want to die. There's an *idée fixe* with a vengeance. . . . And on the other hand . . .

—On the other hand, there's a syllogism to prove them wrong. Socrates . . .

—If there were only a syllogism! . . . But it's fascinating to note that the mind doesn't know how to think of death! Except as an accident, even a scandal.

—That's because it can't form a concept of life either, since death is only a characteristic property of life. Life, in fact, is just some sort of weird swarming process, entirely confined to a surface crust twelve or fifteen thousand meters thick. . . .

—Mere ectoderm. . . .

—Yes, of course. . . . Anything that amuses is superficial. And accidental. Life has the quality of an accident . . . which has created some laws for itself.

—Yes. . . . And on that thin layer there's life, death . . . entries and exits. The fundamental law is statistical. No life without death—a statistical equilibrium. . . .

—And that's where you come in, Doctor.

—I try.

—The intelligence is incapable of grasping life, and the same with death. . . . On the other hand, every individual sensibility wants to get its own advantage out of the game. Result: the individual struggles against the law; the intellect strives for life against life; and you doctors are the champions, the strategists, in the struggle of the individual life against the law of life . . . in the mass. . . .

—Meanwhile, the cow's taken to her heels.

—What cow?

—The one who doesn't give a damn about the stars. . . . At least you said so. Not that you know any more about it than I do. . . . And then, what about monkeys? There's an inquisitive animal, if you like.

—Monkeys? . . . Of course they have a more complex cycle. . . . More involved.

—Go on. . . . You haven't the slightest idea what you're going to say next. I've trapped you. . . . You're in a flagrant state of *inspirational deficiency*. . . .

—Not at all. I'm creating . . . something. I'm drawing from myself what I didn't even know I contained.

—You're drawing on something that isn't there. Is that the way to create?

—*Ex nihilo.*

—Wonderful. That nebula is still evolving, I suppose. . . .

—Of course, Doctor.

—Creative Ignorance, Creation from the Void. . . .

—Why, yes; before the Word is before the Beginning. Before . . . the Before!

—The fact is, beginning's always the worst part, whatever the subject. . . .

—Yes. Fortunately, man is not built all in one piece. One part of him is ahead of another. His mouth waters before he begins to eat. It's rather the same with ideas.

—Let's get down to brass tacks. Weren't you just telling me that you had no idea in advance of what you might draw from your brain and serve up for me?

—No exact idea, no. . . . I've a feeling, an inkling . . .

—In what form? What state? A promise, a hope?

—Well, yes. . . . A feeling of getting near. . . . As though . . .

—From underneath? *Sub*?

—No. Not *sub.* . . . Alongside . . . on the shady fringe of my mind at a given moment.

—Fringe? Mind? Moment? . . . It's none too lucid, all this.

—But that's it's very *nature*, not to be lucid. I can't say I have an *inkling* without implying that it must be rather unclear. . . .

—But you can give some clear equivalent for what you feel as an inkling.

—In that case, I'll have to fall back on comparisons.

—Of course!

—Well then . . . I was saying I had an inkling of my thought—or rather, of my next expression of it, on the fringe of my mind at a given moment. . . . Rather as if you groped for and felt some object through a veil. . . .

—A lovely woman, for instance?

—Go on, you . . . you licensed explorer of pneumatic blisses. . . .

—Without illusions, alas. . . . There's a lot to be said for veils.

—By the way, Doctor, I frankly don't understand how doctors, and above all gynecologians——

—*Gynecologists.*

—Gynecologists can still contrive to . . .

—It's a case of keeping to . . . a timetable. . . .

—Wonderful. . . . So they work in two phases, separating the professional from the . . .

—Purely functional phase.

—You must admit that hands are a really extraordinary appliance. . . . In the morning, professional . . .

—And *by appointment.* . . .

—And in the evening—functional! . . . It's wonderful. They're the all-purpose grippers!

—But what about the mind?

—It begins and ends in the finger tips.

—Yes, and in the meanwhile you dodge my questions. You hedge with every sort of shady quibble. . . . And I've got to listen.

—You're a splendid listener.

—It's an essential, and—I may say—very testing part of my profession. . . . I'm listening to you now, waiting for what you will draw from your mind, and I'm still waiting. . . .

—You need to stir me up a bit. . . .

—So you want me to be an irritant, is that it? I'm here to aid your delivery, am I? . . .

—Oh, Doctor! . . . Well, why not? . . . A man is nothing until something or other stimulates him to certain effects, or products, that surprise even him—for good or bad. A man devoid of stimulus is in a state of void. . . . For instance, whenever I see a passer-by, I often think of all the joy, all the suffering, he carries along with him, in a state of potential. . . .

—Suffering, especially.

—To be made actual on the slightest pretext. . . . In a way, we all carry the sum of our liabilities, invisibly inscribed in our flesh. . . .

—And what about potential ideas! . . .

—And memories! . . . You know, Doctor, I thought about this so much at one time that I invented a word, a name, to cover this capacity for feelings and creations. . . .

—Oh ho! So you've rigged up a modest terminology of your own.

—Yes.

—I had the honor of assisting at the birth of *Omnivalence*, and *Nebula*: can't I meet the whole little family?

—No, no, no. . . . I simply rig up my little terminology

to suit the needs of the moment—but I usually reserve the terms for my own personal ends. . . . They're the tools in my private workshop. I manufacture my products only for myself: they are as individual and as adaptable as possible to my own way of thinking and putting things together.

—You certainly have some pride. . . .

—In what way? Do you think Crusoe was any prouder than the next? I'm an intellectual Robinson Crusoe.

—Well, if that isn't pride! . . . Why, it's isolationism in the worst degree.

—Not at all! . . . It simply accepts the fact of isolation. I am separated from others by what they understand and I don't. . . .

—And by what *you* understand and they don't?

—Exactly. It's the same with everybody. . . . Only perhaps I feel it more acutely—and more directly.

—All right, Mr. Crusoe. . . . And since we are pretty well on an island here, I can serve as a sort of Man Friday? . . . Good. Now what about that word, that name? . . .

—My name for all that inner potentiality that we were talking about is: the *IMPLEX.*

—What a splendid name! Most suggestive. I'm not quite sure what it's suggestive *of*—certainly a whole lot of things. It's a hold-all. We'll have to open up the *Implex.* But wait a moment. Does this Implex of yours amount to any more than what vulgar, common mortals, the masses, philosophers, psychologists, psychopaths, the non-Crusoes—the herd, in fact—call quite simply and crudely the "unconscious" or the "subconscious."

—Do you want me to pitch you into the sea?. . . Don't you know I detest such dirty words? . . . And anyhow, it isn't the same thing at all. They are meant to signify some inconceivable hidden springs of action—at times they stand for sly little inner goblins, marvelous tricksters who can guess riddles, read the future, see through brick walls, and carry on the most amazing industry inside our hidden workings. . . . I don't want to go into all that at present. . . . No, the *Implex* is not an *activity*. Quite the contrary. It's a *capacity*: our capacity for feeling, reacting, doing, and understanding . . . individual, inconstant, more or less known to us . . . but always imperfectly and indirectly (like the sense of tiredness)—and very often misconstrued. To all that we must add our capacity for resistance. . . . And among these possible variations on the possible, some are daily, some are yearly . . .

—Monthly for ladies.

—Naturally. . . . Now, to take an example: think of any verb. The verb *to walk*.

—I'll go along. . . .

—Go through all its moods and tenses.

—*I walk, you walk*. . . . Is there a catch in this somewhere?

—No. . . . Go on. . . . But keep to the first person.

—*I walk, I was walking, I walked, I have walked, I shall walk* . . .

—Do you see?

—No . . . I'm still walking.

—What! You can't see how it varies the Implex? *I walk, I shall walk*. Can't you feel the change of state? . . .

—Reaction negative.

—And even so, the standard conjugations of the verb are far from complete.

—You think they're below par?

—Well. . . . The popular conception divides time into three states: *Past, Present, Future*.

—Nothing new so far.

—Now you can stick your . . . scalpel anywhere you like into chronology. The point you choose as *present* always has its own relative *past* and *future*. Which means an infinity of——

—All right. And then?

—One could go on dividing up. . . . But I'll make it short. The verb offers us only a very restricted range of expressions. It has only five or six colors, which won't blend together, to express infinite shades of meaning: and that's why certain locutions are added to it, to enrich our store a little. . . . Thus, if you stick the point of the *present* into the actual moment . . .

—I'm sticking it in. . . . But I'll be hanged if——

—But it's childishly simple, Doctor. . . . You stick it in, and proceed to create . . .

—I can't feel I'm creating anything. . . .

—You create the present tense of the present, which you express as: *I am in process of* . . .

—What? . . . Sounds like Molière.

—And you create by the same stroke. . . .

—What a scalpel it must be!

—You create the future tense of the present: *I am just about to* . . .

—Explode.

—And so on. The present tense of the present of the present tense, the present tense of the future of the past pluperfect, and so on. . . . You could refine on that. A mathematician could. . . .

—It's the end of the end of the end of the . . .

—There you are! You're into the way of it. You've started exponentiating all by yourself.

—The hell with it!

—To sum up, what I signify by *Implex* is that by which

and in virtue of which we remain contingent, conditional. . . . I mean *we* in the gross, and *we* in particular. . . .

—Wait, give me time to pull my scalpel out and catch up with you. . . . I'm out of breath. . . .

—For instance . . . think of a muscle. . . .

—Ah, muscles! Now I know where I am. Let's have a look at this muscle.

—It can only do two things: stretch, or contract.

—What more can it want?

—It has a very limited implex.

—The fact is, its outlook is not very wide.

—Whatever happens, it can only say: *Short, long; long, short.*

—Force needs no refinement.

—No good pricking it, electrifying it, or teasing it in any other way—is there?

—True. It sticks to its own little routine.

—And now the retina. . . . Its only implex is a certain limited range of lights and colors. . . . Whatever strikes it can only register as light. You could easily define it by a pretty little motto in Latin. . . .

—Wait a minute. . . . What about memory? There's an Implex for you, surely?

—It's the prize exhibit. . . . But, unfortunately . . .

—What?

—It resists investigation. . . . To think we know less than nothing about that almighty and indefinable property. . . .

—Nothing? You're going a bit far. Evidently you're no reader. . . . There are whole libraries on the subject.

—That's just what I mean by saying we know nothing. And in any case it may even be an illusion to try to think of it in itself. . . . No good trying to define it with reference to our notion of the past: we simply refer it back to itself.

—But why try to define it? We all know what it is. . . .

—Yes . . . whenever we talk of it . . . indirectly. When we use the word without stopping to think . . . we hop across the ditch by a plank safely enough. But it's no good trying to pause on that plank, or starting up a little dance on it. If we try to halt at the idea of memory, consider what it really is, at the heart . . . of consciousness, at that "sunspot," that point of intensity and activity where ideas and questions find . . . or seek . . . or receive the maximum concentration, the maximum action upon . . .

—On what, may I ask?

—On the . . . *intellectual* implex, my dear sir.

—Bravo!

—Which means, on the greatest possible number of connections and associations.

—And that's where we place and try to hold this problem of memory, only to find we produce no useful result?

—Exactly. Yes, Doctor, at the very point where, normally, we understand a thing most deeply, we have to acknowledge that we understand nothing at all in this case.

—Amazing. You talk about these things—this heart of consciousness, this most sensitive point of our being at its most intense, as if you were *there*. . . . You're a highly imaginative type.

—Can't help it, Doctor. I'm talking to you as frankly as I may. As I said, my mental life is like Crusoe's.

—And what if I told you that *that* is a nearly classic case of schizophrenia?

—Well, I would conduct Schizophrenia in person to the *fovea centralis* of my mind, to see what I ought to think of her. . . . Anyway, I don't mind. . . . Mentally, I live on my own island! I've told you twice. I'm a Crusoe. With my home-made bow and arrows, I shoot down what birds I can—when there are any.

—And there usually are, I suppose?

—The sky of the mind swarms with them, parrots in particular. They have to be killed off first of all . . . before catching and taming the others.

—So you're a parrot hunter? . . . You must work long hours, in that case?

—Often enough I do, Doctor. And you've been raising flocks of them for me.

—I have? . . . In what sense, what do you mean by parrots?

—Oh Lord. . . . I mean three words out of every six, pretty well. All the words that fail to survive that central scrutiny . . . intact.

—How do you mean?

—Let's see. . . . Suppose you were placing some object or solution or other under your microscope.

—Yes.

—You bring it into focus. You see . . . whatever it may be . . . no matter.

—Yes.

—You proceed from one magnification to a higher one, and then to another. . . .

—All right.

—And you find that the image you get is more and more blurred. The more you do what you can to *fix* it, the vaguer it grows. . . . And there you are. The nebula gets more . . . nebulous!

—And so I find a parrot under my microscope?

—Why, yes. . . .

—And this is the way you behave to poor little words?

—It's the correct way of approaching them: a way of finding out their *real* value in the service of any strict intellectual inquiry. There are contraindications for so many words. Having learned the words, we repeat them, thinking they have a meaning we can . . . utilize: but such words are the creation of habit, and they cannot be used as guaranteed elements in any accurate mental construction or operation without their making it null and void.

—But you are using the word *Mind*?

—That's a shriekingly obvious old parrot, yes. . . . But note, first, that I'm talking to you. . . .

—Thanks for the compliment.

—Don't mention it. One has to make a distinction between general application and a more perceptive usage where a certain strictness——

—Is strictly essential. And then?

—Secondly: terms of this particular kind——

—For external application only! . . .

—Exactly . . . are distinguished for me by a little sign which marks them as strictly *provisional*.

—What a man! You know, I think you're in a highly strung condition. You ought to have a change, it seems to me, take a holiday from all this precision hunting. . . . Don't you feel a bit overwrought? I mean it. . . .

—Yes. I am a little . . . tired.

—How do you sleep?

—About five hours daily on an average.

—It's not a lot.

—But I sleep deeply. And I think that compensates. A short deep sleep must be worth at least as much as a longer light one.

—Perhaps. Do you eat well?

—When I like the cooking.

—And what about . . . the rest?

—You certainly are inquisitive.

—The rest is silence?

—I'm telling you, you're too inquisitive.

—Then let's forget about how to deal with the rest, if you'd rather not talk about it. . . . But I'm warning you. I tell you again, I think you're very highly strung. You ought to let up on that homemade bow of yours, and give the parrots a holiday. . . . Precision may be all very pretty, but it only applies to *solid bodies*. Rigid rules of metallurgy, clear-cut mechanisms, flush contacts, exact coincidences—those are the province of precision tools. But seriously, you mustn't make the same demands on a creature of flesh and blood. Our equipment—nerves, arteries, and so forth—wears itself out if it tries to emulate things that are solidly themselves, and the relationships between indestructible objects.

—You're a sound adviser, Doctor. . . . But this is what I live by. I'm dying of something else. . . .

—You don't look all that dead to me. You gambol about among the rocks like a goat: you battle around with words, for and against, like a devil possessed: working wholesale slaughter among the cockatoos. . . . Nothing alarming in all this. But you go too far. Relax, I tell you, relax. . . .

—I have to burn something up. . . .

—Could it be that you have some personal . . . bothers that you struggle with and encourage at the same time—in your heart of hearts?

—Everybody has. . . .

—Yes, but you're eaten alive. . . .

—Some truth in that.

—You're badly bitten. That's obvious.

—My only remedies for it are mental sharpness and agility.

—I can't exactly define the disease; but I'm afraid the remedies are even worse.

—I don't think so. Every organism has its own defensive weapons.

—My, aren't you captious. . . . Some people take bromides. Some take to alcohol. Others make friends with opium and its distinguished cousins. And others go out and . . . celebrate. I won't mention, except for the record, the rest who go in for shooting, drowning, hanging by the bell rope, and suchlike heroic sedatives. . . . But I've never before met up with an anxiety case who chose to try and cure himself by this sort of quasi-geometrical, chronic, and compulsive analysis. . . . In any case, Logic is in rather bad odor, medically speaking. . . . There are lots of far too consequential thinkers among the anxiety cases and the paranoids.

—But, Lord help us, I'm not an anxiety case!

—Tut tut tut tut!

—I certainly am not. . . . Maybe I'm anxious . . . but not an "anxiety case." . . .

—*Distinguo*. . . . I'd be ready to swear that you're ready to chop logic with——

—Yes, I distinguish. That's my natural . . . property!

—There you go. Firing at parrots again.

—Let me distinguish: I maintain there's an anxiety per se, limitless, and so far as events and exterior circumstances are concerned, causeless. It can be seen very clearly in some people who, as the saying goes, have "everything to make them happy."

—True enough. I'm sorry to say it. But it's true enough.

—But it isn't at all my case. I am anxious . . . to the same degree that a man whose throat is being squeezed is . . . asthmatic. Leave go, and he's cured.

—Right . . . but wait. . . . Some people's throats need only a very tiny pressure. They feel they're choking if you so much as lift your hand. They . . . they're exaggerators. Their nervous systems are one jump ahead of the beat. Now you look to me as if——

—May heaven stand witness. I'd like nothing more than to be exaggerating. . . .

—And what follows? I'm not at all sure that . . . your anxiety——

—Relative! . . .

—Relative anxiety. All right. . . .

—Relative, natural, reasonable! . . .

—All right, all right. . . . I'm not so sure that between your relative, natural, reasonable—and so on—anxiety, and the other, the——

—Essential. . . .

—All right, the essential variety—there isn't . . . an all-too-easy transition. . . . That's what I want to warn you against.

—Everything's possible, Doctor. No doubt I contain all the elements of a classic anxiety case. . . .

—Good. . . . Here we are, back at the Implex. . . .

—And what about your own case? . . . When one thinks of the probable quantity of ideas and acts residing potentially "within us" (in a "latent," which is to say, inconceivable, state), waiting to form successive combinations whose emergence into the actual is what makes us—what we are! Among these, there must be some, of course, that are more frequent, more easily renewable than others; they are familiar to us, they constitute our "personality," they define it, make it credible, conceivable to us as an entity—which can be isolated, is indestructible, a constant, eternal, and independent to the highest degree. . . . But it seems to me that these profound inner connections, this knowledge of our "selves" can be reduced or resolved into organic sensations, appetencies, revulsions, of which a definitive table could be drawn up for every one of us.

—Like the questionnaires in young girls' autograph albums: "Your favorite color?" . . . "Your favorite perfume?"

—Exactly. . . . But changes take place in these connections. Haven't you noticed how tastes alter with age?

—Mmm . . . Children don't care for oysters, or truffles.

—And yet what could be more *personal* than our tastes?

—Our distastes!

—Even more so. . . . At any moment, I coincide with what I tend to perceive. At any given moment in his life each of us is a system of . . . potential attractions and repulsions, as well as of . . . inner sensations of force and resistance. But the pattern varies endlessly, with time.

—In fact, with anything at all?

—Nevertheless . . . that changing pattern is what we most essentially *are*!

—Are you fond of tripe?

—Agh! . . . I loathe the stuff!

—Well . . . and what about coffee?

—I live on it.

—Good. . . . Now just try to imagine that in . . . say . . . three years' time you found you had gradually acquired a fondness for tripe, and an aversion for coffee.

—True enough, alas, all things are possible. . . .

—And what about your personality?

—On this point it will consist of a memory—of my

former passion for coffee and my loathing for tripe.

—You agree that something is left, then?

—Mmm. . . . A chance memory, with nothing else to support it, is at the mercy of——

—But suppose, instead of tripe and coffee, I had instanced something else. . . . For example, if I'd asked you whether some more deep-rooted and violent appetite—one that occupies the mind, not only at mealtimes, but day and night, for months on end—perhaps for years—an appetite both obsessive and . . .

—Embittered. . . .

—Yes, and . . . in fact, all-compelling: if I asked you whether that too would be liable to the same slow diminution and extinction . . .

—It seems impossible; and yet I quite agree, it's true.

—Aha!

—Now may I ask you a question, Doctor? As a medical man, what do you think is the origin of this variety of tastes? Why do I not like tripe, and how could I change my mind about it?

—Nobody knows. . . . Which means I can tell you! It's a question of metabolism! . . . You know . . . biochemistry, internal secretions, the action of chemical disturbances on the nerve cells. . . . Throw in a few reflexes, and associations of ideas . . .

—And serve hot.

—Yes, and there you are.

—So we very appropriately take cover in the undergrowth of small, smaller, smallest. At about the millionth of a millimeter, all becomes clear. . . . There's plenty of room in that area. It seems that if all the inter- and intra-atomic spaces could be suppressed, a man's body could be popped into a matchbox.

—Oh well, I was simply summing up . . .

—The current scientific view. . . . In the present case, you can put that, too, into a matchbox.

—What do you expect? I'm sorry, but we're in a bog. It's fearfully complex. After all, there's no reason why a living being should be able to arrive at a true picture of life. . . . A while since, when we were enjoying the fine view we have here, and contrasting it with a remote close-up of the dog's life we lead in Paris, with all that hugger-mugger of things, people, and notions seen in perspective, you mentioned the Greeks.

—Yes. An easy illusion. The name is a sort of myth, evoking in itself a model way of life . . . physically agreeable, or else gloriously instinctive, along with a twin ideal of intellectual rigor and intellectual freedom. But we put a good deal of our own wishful thinking into it. . . .

—Well, the mention of it gave me an unpleasant feeling. Everything I've been able to master seemed reduced to . . . almost nothing. The very vocabulary of science struck me suddenly as weird, comic, dated, antique.

—There's one thing that strikes me. To speak only of the biological sciences, people had the highest hopes, forty or fifty years ago. . . . Between 1850 and 1880 evolution, microbes, organic synthesis, histology, had all been taken on. . . . Everything seemed about to converge on some clear-cut concept. . . . There were even hopes of more than that. Quite a few people looked forward to the day when they would see a living jelly detach itself from some solution of absolutely lifeless matter. . . .

—But it's still the case! . . . It's even suggested that by certain effects of radiation, quite unthought-of in those days . . .

—Yes. But I'm talking of hopes. In those days the goal was only a hundred yards off; and now it seems much more like a hundred miles. . . . I'm only speaking, of course, for those who see it in finite terms.

—Hope, said the Doctor, is a theme for variations.

—Hope . . .

—Yes, up with your gun. Down with that bird!

—Hope, I murmured, hope . . .

—Is the heart's best gift from heaven.

—Yes, another illustrious unknown. Even more unknown than an *idée fixe.* In all your volumes of psychology or psychiatry I suspect it's never mentioned. . . . But then I've read them so little, I may be wrong. . . .

—I can't tell you. It's not my department. But I'd be surprised if . . . it may well be that it comes up for consideration —under some technical name they've found for it.

—I'm sadly afraid . . .

—You mean you despair of hope?

—I greatly fear. . . . You see, I've noticed (or think I've noticed) that the simplest facts, the most frequent, the most anciently observed and classified, are the ones most neglected by our writers. Don't you agree that the emphasis on pathology, which almost inevitably dominates all research, must lead to . . .

—Distortion?

—I hardly dared say it. . . . And to gaps. . . . And even to useless, misdirected labor. . . .

—It's possible. But remember, my dear man, that without that emphasis, there might never have been any research. And then look at the discoveries prompted by pathology! . . . The fact that life is still possible under conditions more or less debased, diminished, or precarious: the struggle it puts up, the interchanges, the readjustments—all that is quite as illuminating, say, as the alterations of equilibrium in a physicochemical system. . . . Not to mention the revelations afforded by diagnosis, autopsy . . .

—Yes. *Oportet haereses esse.* There have to be abnormalities and illnesses. All the same, I can't get rid of that notion I was mentioning.

—Go on.

—I will risk the impression that physiology doesn't play the part it ought to.

—Really? But wonderful work is being carried out . . .

—Yes. In the schools.

—I grant you that perhaps not enough is being done . . . but where do we find the time? We live in a demanding age. We've got to master as quickly as possible all the knowledge we can utilize and turn into cash.

—I'm not talking about practitioners only. And I'm speaking as a layman. But . . . where do I get this feeling? . . . It's simply that I've never anywhere discovered—I mean in any of the books that have come my way—any trace of a tendency, or will, to build up a complete working idea of the living being. . . . I mean, an idea of its functioning as a whole. . . . I find wonderful analyses of particular functions, but no effort at synthesis. . . . It's rather as if the physicists had sworn to make separate studies of optics, mechanics, heat, chemistry. . . . But *they*'ve tried to establish connections. Now do you believe that an organism is less of a . . . unity than the universe?

—You're asking for the moon, my dear man. . . .

—I know! That's my vocation. . . . Maybe I carry it to extremes. My idea, false or otherwise, is that physiology in the eighteenth century was less . . . departmentalized . . .

—But they went in for metaphysics. . . .

—"Mechanics," rather. . . . Think of Barthez. . . .

—Metaphysics, metaphysics!

—Wait. Let me put in a word from personal experience. It will illustrate my little thesis better than any argument. Ten—or twenty—times I've asked ten or twenty doctors—or neurologists, if you'd rather—whether there was such a thing as a systematic table of the known reflexes.

—I certainly don't know of one.

—There you are!

—But it's all to be found in the theses on physiology, pathology, in the casebooks and so forth. Look up Babinski, Foix, Froment.

—But do you think it's "scientific"—a hiatus as big as that? I'm putting the question as ingenuously as possible, what I mean is: if you think—*quite simply*—of a living, functioning being, taking note that its functions can be resolved into a series of *modifications*, the most obvious of these being the reflexes, it has often occurred to me that if *I* specialized in the study of living organisms, I would need that systematic table, to work over it, to test my subjects with the various combinations and conflicts . . . of all these elementary but extraordinary responses. . . . It's a highly particularized field of action, in which time plays an essential role. Now where's the metaphysics in that?

—I can see it in your eyes, Mr. Reflex Hunter! They're darting lightnings of sacred rage. . . . You're getting violently worked up about the nonexistence of this Table of the Laws . . . the urgent need for which I confess I fail to see.

—Wait, then. Let me take you up in your own field. Your specialty. Your department.

—I'm ready for you!

—Therapy itself is supposed to be changing values.

—I've heard it said.

—What cured in 1880 kills in 1890.

—Yes. There's a ten-year cycle approximately. It's a question of fashion, partly, I agree. But even more, it's a question of progress.

—But what if there were something else?

—What else?

—Some inner transformation. . . .

—Of what, exactly?

—Of man himself? . . . A transformation of the . . . requirements of our cells—and so of their reactions, too?

—As a Robinson Crusoe, there's simply nothing you'll deny yourself, is there?

—That is the immense and inalienable privilege of ignorance. . . . I can try every method. . . .

—And I'm your guinea pig.

—Turn and turn about. . . . Well then, Doctor, do you know what you ought to do? I can guarantee fame as a result.

—What do I want with fame?

—The sense of glory!

—Evidently you don't know what it is. I've handled a few euphorics. . . . They're always in need of winding up.

—Yes, but wait. . . . Is there such a thing as a History of Therapy?

—Still another book you're after? . . . I don't think so.

—Write one.

—Me? . . . God forbid.

—You could keep to the nineteenth century, and what we've seen of this one so far. . . .

—But you've no idea of the work that . . .

—I bet you anything that the results would be remarkable. . . .

—No, sir . . . a hundred times no. Why should I set about something I've never dreamed of doing? I'm a doctor. General practitioner. I practise, and that's that! . . . No theorizing. No books to write. I've enough to do with my patients.

—What about the disease of activity? And that article in *Brain*?

—That would be a mere pastime. And anyhow, I repeat, I've never had a notion of writing books. . . .

—Nor I, neither. . . . And yet . . .

—It isn't my affair, it's not my line. . . .

—It's there in your Implex, Doctor. . . . Do you think you know what you'll be doing in a year's time? What I've been saying will start working in you.

—In my *Sub*-something-or-other? I'm not worried.

—Nor I. I know all too well that we can never guess the results of everything we happen to hear. It's not impossible . . . it's most probable that everything affects us, that nothing happens, however imperceptible, but it germinates, and one fine day it produces an effect in our mind that surprises us, and whose origin we can neither conceive nor identify.

—That's the exploded theory of impregnation. A white woman marries a Negro, buries him, marries a white, who makes her bring forth a whole string of pickaninnies. . . . General amazement!

—There you have a perfect image of autosuggestion. You'd better watch out. You'll be giving birth before you know it.

—Now you are going a bit too far! . . . Trying to work your suggestions on me. . . .

—It's my turn now! . . . It's the old conflict of amateur versus professional. Like that tale of the contest between the sorcerers.

—What contest? What's all this about sorcerers?

—Don't you remember? . . . That Arabian story. . . .

—I don't know what you are talking about.

—It's a splendid story. . . . But, come to think of it . . . it has a parallel in the Bible. Which may be a variant or a corruption of the original.

—The Bible? I still don't follow. . . . And between you and me, it's just possible I've never read the Bible. . . .

—It's quite interesting. Oddly assembled. . . . But wonderful in parts.

—So what happened?

—There was a certain Pharaoh. With a college of Magi attached to his suite.

—Poor wretch.

—Along comes Moses.

—All right. If nobody comes along there's no story.

—True enough. You could build up a whole formula for fiction out of that.

—No good. Let's get back to Moses.

—The moment he arrives, Moses astonishes the king with a series of miracles. . . . He changes water into blood, kills fishes by remote control. . . .

—Not bad. . . . It sounds like the shape of wars to come!

—The sorcerers are stung into retaliation. . . .

—Jealousy, of course! . . . It's always the same. I suppose they were the bureaucrats?

—That's right. . . .

—It must be a true story.

—So Pharaoh decrees a competition. . . .

—How did he have the nerve! . . . Against his own bureaucracy?

—It seems it was a . . . war of parasites.

—I thought so . . . a case of who's going to batten on poor old Pharaoh.

—No, no. I mean parasites *qua* parasites. . . . Parasites in the *basic sense*, if I can put it that way. Frogs, grasshoppers . . .

—But they aren't parasites. . . .

—Mosquitoes . . .

—The malarial anopheles! Poor Pharaoh obviously had the shakes.

—Moses, for his part, was as lavish as he could be with plagues and catastrophes.

—A model statesman. . . . So he won? . . .

—But that isn't the tale I really wanted to tell. The Arabian version is much more to the point. . . .

—You're a one for droll stories! . . .

—Part of my trade. . . . In the Arab story, once again it's a question of a magic duel—a case of which side will devour the other.

—I see. Vital competition. A shorthand version of Biology.

—*And* Literature.

—And all the rest.

—In short, one magician turns into a cat to eat the other, who had turned into a rat . . .

—Down with vermin.

—Yes, but the rat turns into a tiger. . . .

—And the cat, into a lion!

—Naturally. But the tiger turns into a flea. . . .

—Bravo! But the lion turns into a microbe. . . . Do you know what this reminds me of?

—Everything in life, Doctor.

—Just think: a few years back someone put my name down on an election roster. Doctors are rather liable, you know. . . . So I found myself a candidate for the local council. Ward No. 20. . . . My dear man, I found I had to pile it on thicker from one minute to the next.

—You had a very wily mage as your opposite number?

—A pharmacist—a holy terror! From poster to poster, from meeting to meeting, the pace got hotter and fiercer. . . . We were spouting flames, and showering promises right and left. . . . And the mudslinging—it was delightful! . . . And the names we called each other! . . .

—So he ate you up?

—No. He just squashed me.

—The devil. . . .

—Oh, he's a very worthy fellow. The next year he was doing all he could to get me decorated. . . .

—What on earth did you think you were doing, going into politics?

—I don't know myself.

—There you are. How do you know it won't be the same with that History of Therapy?

—That's quite a different thing.

—Could you have guessed, three minutes ago, that we'd now be discussing Pharaoh and political infighting?

—It's true we can't foresee ourselves all that clearly.

—Perhaps there's no such thing as "Ourselves," outside the . . . instant. . . .

—Metaphysics again!

—Wait a minute, Doctor. Didn't this pharmacist drive you into making some rather overhectic assertions? Not to mention promises and statements that you can't re-read without . . .

—Do you suppose I ever look back at them?

—All the same, it prompted some things that you never thought you had in you. And so you can't deny you have . . . an Implex.

—My Implex must have been a bit overloaded. When it was all over, when I'd dissolved the committees, paid the expenses, and expressed my gratitude to my one hundred and thirteen faithfuls . . .

—What? Only a hundred and thirteen votes?

—As against two thousand and forty-five, at the first count. . . .

—And you declared the man was a rogue, a traitor . . .

—He had the nerve to suggest I had certain proclivities . . .

—But you don't know if, the day after tomorrow . . .

—No, I can vouch for it. Under that head, I'm as sure of myself as I am of——

—You are of the Universe. . . . But no more than that. . . .

—I don't give a hang for the Universe. . . .

—For which I owe you my infinite thanks, Doctor. . . .

—Why?

—Because the *Universe* . . .

—Lord help us! . . . He's spied another parrot! . . .

—This one's the Parrot of all parrots. . . . *Psittacus psittacorum.*

—And a veteran, to boot! Old in the teeth . . .

—And married.

—No, really?

—To Dame Parrot Nature. . . . Magnificent birds . . . dazzling words in mile-high capital letters . . . they people the sky of the mind. And their only strength is . . . words.

—So you pop them under your microscope. . . .

—Naturally. Not long ago I was discussing the Universe with a most sapient sage. . . . Stars, atoms, spaces, waves, transmutations, and so forth. You know . . . all the current stock-in-trade. . . .

—A mixed bag.

—Yes. A bit of everything. Symbols, unimaginable entities; chance and necessity in a more or less monstrous state of copulation; integers that annihilate all decimal figures;

your statistics of mortality taking on an astronomical rate of interest. . . .

—There are too many facts, you know. . . . No one knows how to add up all our winnings in the lottery of experiment. The deductions all talk at once. . . .

—Resulting in mental confusion. . . .

—Which gets worse confounded with the confusion of reality.

—So, I was talking about the Universe with my sage; and suddenly I said, "What do you mean, *exactly*, by the word?"

—I can just hear you!

—Well, he hesitated for quite some time. . . . His face took on an . . . indefinable expression. . . .

—Just what was required. . . .

—He looked away beyond me. . . . Suppressed me, I might say. . . .

—A good idea. Much the best approach.

—And then he touched down again from that world . . .

—Where nothing can be situated.

—And he said: "It's a sphere . . ."

—Whose center is everywhere and whose——

—No. "A sphere . . . of such a kind that . . . nothing exists outside it."

—I bet you a hundred thousand dollars you weren't satisfied.

—You're a rich man.

—So you see?

—What, Doctor?

—That you have an *idée fixe*, that I've located it, and that I can guess your every move, just as I choose! . . . I can manipulate you ad lib!

—Nothing of the sort! . . . It's not an *idée fixe*, it's just an *omnivalent* . . . hang it all!

—So here we are again.

—And on this artificial rock we'll set about that sorcerers' duel!

—I turn into a psychopathologist! . . .

—I'm a logician. . . .

—I get you locked up. . . .

—And I——

—Help! Help! To the rescue, my two hundred and thirteen adherents . . .

—You're cheating. . . . You said a hundred and thirteen a minute ago.

—Lord Almighty. . . . It's the electoral stakes all over again.

—No. Heavens, no. . . . Electoral stakes, polemics, personal abuse. . . . All that, my dear Doctor, belongs to the hideous Universe of the Automatic.

—True enough. I was saying, a minute since—or rather, I was going to say that when the whole affair was over . . .

—All expenses paid up, the helpers thanked, and the committee dissolved . . .

—Yes. . . . I had the feeling of being released from a dream, of being "myself" once more.

—So dreams exist?

—In exactly the same way as the Universe does. . . .

—Beware automatism! . . .

—There's no way of doing without it.

—Agreed. But I fear its advances. . . .

—In what way do you think it's making advances?

—Uniformity is now the order of the day. Its ramifications are growing far too luxuriant. . . . All races imitate each other. Capital cities differ only in what is left of their past. . . . And anyhow, there is an irresistible force at work, that will go on working in the same direction.

—Meaning?

—A positive intellectual discipline, imprinted in the mind by the use or abuse of scientific procedures.

—There always has been a mental discipline imposed on the vast majority.

—Yes. There was a mystical or metaphysical discipline . . . but it was inculcated. I'm afraid ours, positive and self-evident as it is, will come to diminish in all human minds the possible sum total of . . . Sovereign Good. . . .

—What's that you're saying?

—Yes. I mean the quantity . . . or rather the degree of liberty of the human mind—which is the Sovereign Good.

—I confess I don't follow at this point. I'd have said, on the contrary . . .

—No, I insist. . . . You can extricate yourself from laws of external origin—untie all the knots, cut through all the threads that bind from without. That is always possible. . . . *But* it's almost impossible to free yourself from habits of mind which are as fully justified by experience as thinking possibly can be, and justified, moreover, by critical investigation, whenever they are put to the test. The power of modern man is based on "objectivity." But look closer and you'll see that this power is possessed by objectivity in itself—and not by man himself. He is becoming the tool—or slave—of what he has discovered or evolved . . . a *way of looking*.

—A method. . . . But what if this is the right way? If it's the threshold, the goal where centuries of groping have finally arrived—and ought to arrive?

—All very well . . . but beware automatism!

—You mean to say you set out as a parrot-slayer, you drive on and on towards more and more precision, and then you switch direction!

—No. . . . Anyhow, there's no such thing as a mind at one

with itself. It would no longer be a mind. But listen a moment. Allow me to stray awhile into the thicket of ethics.

—Off you go! . . .

—Now suppose some nondescript authority or other——

—Aren't they all?

—Established a code of morals, an index of moral values: good and evil succinctly defined, every imaginable action being given its ethical coefficient, whether positive or negative——

—Or nil. . . . But this is nothing new. . . .

—Not quite. But suppose that by some equally ordinary procedure, all-powerful mass suggestion, child training, an educational system as effective as our present one is the reverse, bearing the same relationship to ours as our material equipment bears to that of the most backward races . . . a condition was attained whereby the *good deed* became a completely reflex act, almost automatic . . . and the *bad deed* became impossibly difficult, painful even to think of. . . .

—What then?

—Well, there would no longer be any *virtue*, would there? Doing good would have no value. On the other hand, evil would be priced out of the market. . . .

—Splendid for everyone.

—But our moralists would all go frantic. . . .

—Who would worry about that? And anyhow, why? The moralists would surely be in clover. No more sin, no more backsliding, no more crimes. . . .

—Far from it! It isn't virtue they're after. . . . It's the pains you have to inflict on yourself to achieve it!

—What a bunch of sadists!

—No. They're simply moral athletes. The effort is all. Virtue is strife. Every force drives against some other force. But if I flee evil . . . the way my hand jumps from something burning—if the chance of doing good has the same effect on me as that produced upon the salivary glands by . . .

—The taste of tripe. . . .

—Horrors! No . . . of some delicious fruit. In that case human conduct, behavior——

—Mores.

—I loathe that word. A useless neologism.

—Finicky! . . . It's an excellent term.

—In short, all I mean is that human conduct, once it could be automatically directed into the . . . paths of virtue, would no longer be of any interest.

—Tell that in the law courts. They'd be interested.

—But surely you can see that the reduction of ethics to a set of mechanical reflexes would undermine the whole moral world? . . .

—It's only a half-world . . .

—Would dry up the unknown source of that "elemental energy" which . . .

—Which what?

—Which . . . well, which inspires all action that appeals to the ideal. And it would wipe out all those fine shades of discrimination that are born of internal conflicts.

—Oh, would it!

—Our private casuistries, the ingenious inventions whereby we deceive ourselves . . .

—If we talk to ourselves, we're bound to tell a lie occasionally.

—Yes . . . lie, contradict, hide from ourselves what we know, and know what we hide. . . . In short, be *too many* for ourselves, and live . . . on several planes at once. . . .

—Keeping three or four "wives"—and as many "codes of honor."

—Yes. Maybe. . . . But to go back. Just carry over the

same principle into the intellectual world—an airtight organization, an infallible "method," absolute and inflexible—and then! You can see already what a slaughter of imaginative enterprise in our own time . . .

—You think so? . . . But what more do you want? . . . My good man, go and take a look at the beach. . . . Hydroplanes everywhere overhead; the sand black with . . . sunburned muscles; old dames dressed up as Harlequins; Venuses and Adonises playing bat and ball. . . .

—Sorry, that's nothing but mimetism. Mass production of the grotesque. All those whimsies are the order of the day.

—One trousered lady breeds a thousandfold. . . .

—You've an aptitude for poetry, Doctor!

—And you certainly dabble your fingers in medicine!

—So does everyone. It's a sort of autosuggestion—a direct result of the fact that one is mortal. Well, this universal imitation applies on the beach as elsewhere. All those people go in for peeling their skins quite automatically. They obey the rule. . . . But I was talking about the intellect. . . .

—And you say it's getting mechanized, too. . . . But open your eyes, my dear man, never have people evolved such hair-raising theories as now.

—Where do you mean?

—Everywhere. . . . In writing above all, as is natural . . . and then in painting. They certainly serve up some horrors—with theories to match. . . .

—Lord, yes. . . . The product has to have directions on the packet.

—You'll excuse my launching into this. It's your department. . . . But all of it seems such mumbo-jumbo. . . . I give up. . . .

—By all means, Doctor. Go right ahead. No offense. . . .

I might have been shocked if you'd thought the opposite. But note this: the more there is of mumbo-jumbo (as you call it), the more automatism prevails—grows more obvious, insistent, and tyrannical.

—How do you make that out?

—Why, it's the same as in politics.

—Like my pharmacist?

—Exactly. If he, your opposite number, howled "Thief!" you roared "Traitor!"

—And off we go! Like the sorcerers' contest. The rat becomes a tiger.

—The cat a lion.

—The tiger a flea.

—The lion a microbe—quite automatically. . . .

—Graphococcus.

—Doctor, there you have modernity in a nutshell. The universal poker game of promises, threats, insults, inventions, and bigger dimensions—the political, economical, technical, literary, military poker game. . . . The race in armaments, improvements, and . . . astonishments.

—But it was always the same. . . .

—Not at this rate of acceleration. And that's the point. Reaction speeds have grown much, much faster. . . . Stronger and stronger, bigger and bigger, quicker and quicker, less and less human—that's the automa tic formula. . . .

—So we live in the reign of Mumbo-Jumbo the Automatic?

—Of course. If the value of a thing is made to depend on the effect of surprise it produces, then its ultimate definition must reside solely in its shock value. . . . Do you realize that it's scarcely more than a century since the novelty of a thing came to be regarded as one of its *positive* attributes?

—Splendid. . . . There's something just right for that History of Therapy. . . . You were implying just now that the human organism itself craved novelty, grew bored with fashionable remedies in a few years, and refused to mend itself unless it was offered some new and unheard-of stimulus.

—It's a fact! Theriac reigned as the supreme cure-all for five or six centuries. And then in thirty years we've witnessed sero-, auto-, photo-, electro-, opo-therapies; and there isn't a metalloid, a metal, an alkaloid, a leaven, a weird molecular combination, a light- or heat-ray, a vegetable, a fruit skin, or a cereal germ, without mentioning insect stings, calves' livers, palpitating pigeon's muscle, sea water, and all the interstitial substances, ovarian, thyroid, adrenal—and even the imperceptibles and imponderables, the vitamins from A to Z, that haven't been called in to attack the human system unawares. Nothing quite so miscellaneous or extravagant has been attempted by writers. . . .

—But, my dear man, it comes to the same thing, the same need. The modern body, like the modern mind, needs shock treatment. Both are . . . philoclastic. And I'm not talking of world events. . . .

—The age of Knockout.

—But you can go further. . . . In the most abstract sciences——

—The sciences? . . . Perhaps so. . . .

—You've an embarrassment of riches. . . . For instance, what more could you want than the "time atom."

—The *chronon*? It has no official existence yet.

—They're thinking about it. . . . And there are plenty of other innovations I've heard discussed—without making head or tail of them, of course. So if I say we are living in the most harebrained of centuries . . .

—And the least individual.

—Never have people had to put up with so many senseless ideas, all so well supported, established!—so uncertain, so easily outmoded, demolished, replaced . . .

—Maybe so. . . .

—You think that's a sign of increasing intellectual cowardice? Of the alarming advances of the automatic?

—But do we mean the same thing by that word? For me, *automatism* signifies some result entirely determined by whatever the initial event may be. The muscle contracts automatically in response to no matter what——

—Stimulus. . . . Omnivalence again!

—An ovule begins to evolve . . .

—Omnivalence!

—And the mind . . . but don't let's go into that. . . . We are at the mercy of everything: more or less carriers of an infinity of possible developments—more or less probable—at times . . . infectious. The terrain is more or less favorable to fertilization. . . .

—Bang . . . off we go with the Implex again. It's automatic.

—I should say so. . . . If a mind never traveled the same road twice . . .

—Now that would be a pretty case. Can't you see it? A patient who could never think of the same thing twice. . . . What a godsend for the psychiatrists!

—*On Disturbances in the Probability Function.* Crown Octavo. With plates. . . .

—A good title. Maybe it indicates a whole new world for psychiatry.

—That poor and wretched cousin to Pathology. It's prey to Schizophrenia. . . .

—But what can you expect? . . . Everything's so difficult. And nothing's more muddled, elusive, indefinable, than the mind itself.

—Do you know what struck me about insanity—in the common application of the word? Studying the mad . . . well, it amounts to comparing one's own, supposedly sane, mind with . . . other minds. . . . It's like observing the planets. . . .

—Comets, rather!

—From an imaginary fixed point of vantage. I did that for a few months.

—Where was this?

—In an asylum. About thirty years ago. . . .

—The devil you did! . . .

—As a mere layman.

—That's what they told you!

—I watched the treatment, followed the daily interviews.

—And so?

—What struck me was that all the disturbances to be seen there, selected, assembled, and concentrated together—the manias, delusions, phobias, and so on—all exist in the so-called normal mind . . . but in a diffused state, intermittent, manageable, disseminated, germinal, and very easily concealed! We are all injected with madness—madness in a state of solution. We, the normal, are in a state of adjustable and fairly stable equilibrium. But given some interference of a cellular or muscular order . . . then all these little isolated irregularities that seemed to be imperceptible, harmless, negligible . . .

—Crystallize. . . . We begin to *flake off* mentally . . .

—Into obvious, staringly obvious symptoms. The euphoric becomes President of the Republic. The fixated forget to be hungry or thirsty. It can happen, too, that extreme inversions of temperament set in . . . though I'm convinced that these were always implicit. There must have been a seed, a secret tendency, awaiting a touch . . .

—He's touched, people say.

—And the merest touch can do a lot. . . . But think of all the people who are not and never will be mad, who are nevertheless weirdly and extravagantly different, according to whether they're alone or in company.

—I won't let you out of my sight. . . .

—The greater the difference, the greater . . . It seems as if another's presence exerts a restraint that maintains the equilibrium. . . . The moment such people are alone——

—The monkey's on the table. . . . It's a reaction.

—Restraint, reaction; . . . simulation, release . . . How queer it is! Ironically enough, simulation, the ability to assume otherness, suddenly becomes an attribute of the sane man, the norm—it's almost a *sine qua non.*

—Hey, presto! You're up to conjuring tricks. . . . And now it's my turn. . . . You claim that all abnormalities are implicit, or exist to a degree . . .

—An *infinitely slight* degree; they shrink and vanish at the least warning. Monkey gets back into his cage, the pocket-size madness scampers out of sight. The distorted, furious, or ecstatic face becomes . . . a façade; the madman dives under, and the mind becomes the showman of a well-conducted person once more.

—Very well. . . . But what about the particular kind of madness which, far from hiding, exploits itself insolently—in defiance of . . . the Universe? . . . The madness that . . . dazzles the beholder?

—Napoleon? So we're always coming back to him. . . .

—Yes, but I mean all the great, poets, artists . . .

—The ones who flake off . . . in masterpieces?

—Yes. What about them?

—It doesn't alter what I said. Or hardly at all. Perhaps what distinguishes them is their action upon the common mass from which they separate out. The mass tends to draw towards them . . . out of curiosity. But if you start introducing exceptions of a superior order . . . this is where I, too, introduce a fresh element.

—You've got a flock of white doves up your sleeve, or a bowl of goldfish?

—No. Simply a memory. Which just fits in here.

—I can see it, the sly little beggar, waiting its chance to make the right entry. Now's its big moment, is that it?

—The sense of fitness is the intelligence of the Implex. . . . Or, if you prefer a more . . . aseptic formula: The sense of fitness is the *tropism* of the Implex.

—Honor is satisfied.

—Which comes to saying that, in a given circumstance, what is most needed is summoned up, attracted by the circumstance itself.

—What more can we ask? . . . You're taking me all the way round the mulberry bush. . . . And then?

—Well, I believe that alongside the development of so-called "morbid" symptoms, we have to envisage the development of another kind, perhaps even rarer. . . . Anyhow, it's not always easy to classify. . . .

—I love the word. It always has such class. I classify, you classify . . .

—A development of the latter kind might be called a *deviation*, or *harmonic excursus*.

—Lordy-lord!

—So you think it should be easy to describe and name these things?

—Let's classificate. What doesn't exist is always easy to name, but very difficult to describe. You're making a gallant effort.

—Doctor, Doctor, be careful now. . . . You mean to say you can't conceive of a state of mental effort completely removed from the mind's ordinary kind of freedom and haphazardness, a state equally opposed to distraction or fixation, and which can only satisfy itself (unless forced to a standstill by fatigue) with the possession of a sort of . . . mental object, which the mind can recognize as the thing it was searching for? . . . And yet—laugh if you like—it *did not know* what the object was which it now recognizes—but there was no mistaking it.

—The call of instinct. . . .

—Right! . . . But it's more than that. . . . No use guffawing, you've made a direct hit, or very nearly. . . . It's something rather better than the voice of instinct, intuition. . . . In fact, I'm not going to tell you what it is. . . .

—That's not very nice of you.

—No. Do you agree that a certain kind of mental labor tends to form or construct . . . or rather, to let a whole order or system take form from a given part, or from given conditions?

—As per Cuvier?

—Oh, roughly, yes. . . . Or again, do you agree that the words "Order" and "Disorder" correspond to something?

—Something very relative.

—Agreed. Well, in this very relative field, most people, the immense majority, venture only timidly; they see in their minds, beyond the first stimulus of curiosity, only certain . . .

beginnings. They scarcely follow these up, connect them as vaguely as possible. Most people's thinking remains largely at this dawning stage. . . . They can't . . . they don't know how to tame their Implex.

—You think so?

—In any case, I'm sure of one thing: nothing could be rarer than the ability to co-ordinate, harmonize, orchestrate, a large number of disparate *parts.* That activity, the creation of order, requires, to my mind, two opposing conditions. . . . It calls for the maintenance, the control—beyond the moment, beyond ordinary time. . . .

—So there's such a thing as extraordinary time? It's certainly an extraordinary notion! . . . It's a case of one damn surprise after another, with you. . . . We never know where we are.

—But why shouldn't there be an extraordinary time? . . . You admit that a space in which a magnetic field is produced has properties which are no longer those of . . . ordinary space?

—Very well. I'll take what's coming.

—All right. So you can hold in suspension, present yet mutually independent, a series of distinct factors.

—And then? . . . My brain's reeling already. . . .

—And then, just as in a liquid medium, left undisturbed, having reached the requisite saturation point . . .

—That's just how I feel.

—A certain pattern takes form . . . a pattern which no longer has anything to do with your volition.

—Then with whose, for God's sake?

—Good heavens . . . with the gods, of course. What is required is submission to a certain constraint: the ability to keep this up, endure it fixedly, so as to give those elements of . . . thought which are present, or in operation, the *liberty* to find their affinities, the *time* to combine together constructively and to assert themselves in the conscious mind . . . or to impose some indefinable *conviction* upon it. . . . Look: suppose we were fully conscious of all the work the eye carries out in adjusting its vision. The aim is to focus clearly. You have several adjustable organs at your disposal for this: a lens of variable thickness; a contractable diaphragm; a whole apparatus for directing and converging. Each of these organs can adapt itself independently. Now, imagine that in order to arrive at that unique complex of mutual adjustments which will ensure clear vision of a certain object, you are compelled to make an acute effort—so acute that very few people can sustain it—an effort so limited in its durability and by its difficulty that the attainment of clear vision takes on the extreme, the exceptional value—the quality of *genius*, which we attribute to the highest mental insight. . . .

—Yes, I see, I see. . . . I agree there's a certain correspondence. . . .

—Doctor, I think you deserve a little story.

—It's been a long wait!

—No, I'm wrong. It's a big story. But very short. I was telling you I had a sudden memory. . . .

—Yes. . . .

—Here it is. . . . It has a certain beauty, and a certain reference to what we were saying.

—And if it hadn't, we could always find one, eh?

—Give ear. . . . About two years ago Einstein came to Paris to give a couple of lectures on his latest researches.

—I'll own I haven't been able to make much of what I've read or heard about his theories.

—That doesn't matter much. . . . In any case, don't worry. . . . Most of his audience could only follow with the greatest difficulty. . . . And they were all specialists, save one. In a nutshell, the question was, what would remain of our Physics if we were to make our observations, experiments, and measurements in a not-very-large laboratory (but larger, say, than an atom) which was free to move ad lib through the Universe? It's assumed that *something*, some residue of our laws—which were discovered and formulated under localized conditions—would subsist, in spite of the displacement of the observer, in spite of the speeds, and even the speed variations, of the flying laboratory. . . . An immense step forward was made when the imaginary observer of our planetary system was transferred from the earth to the sun. But the Theory of Relativity seeks to liberate observation completely from all the effects due to the local determination of its measurements, and to its state of movement. This system of a Physics within a Physics was conceived and built up by Einstein in the form of a Geometry. . . .

—I'm lost already.

—Now wait; here's a very rough image. Imagine a flat sheet of rubber.

—If I must.

—Draw a figure on this sheet.

—I'll draw a triangle.

—Good. Now your triangle has certain properties. . . .

—Heaps of them. . . .

—Now you stretch, twist, and fold your rubber sheet as much as you like. What is left of those properties?

—Damned if I know.

—Something is left. . . . If you've evolved a geometry for the plane triangle you first drew, and if you evolve another geometry to fit one distortion of it, and another for another . . .

—It makes a whole lot of geometries! . . .

—And it isn't too wild a hope to look for those axioms or theorems——

—Which won't distort with each distortion?

—That's right.

—And that's what Einstein means?

—Yes, only much more so. Remember, it's a case of stretching, twisting, and folding . . . the whole of Physics, and Time.

—He's a cool customer! . . . But where's the story? . . . All these preliminaries are a bit on the abstract side for me.

—Here it is. But note first that his aim is no less than to seek out and define the Unity of Nature.

—But who's to prove there's such a thing as unity in nature?

—That precisely is the question I put to Einstein. And he replied: *It's an act of faith.*

—Ouch. . . .

—Yes. It seems that he *hopes* to isolate, from all the results of physical research, a certain formula which will represent the most . . . *objective* view man can reach. . . . Remember that the radius of knowledge extends from the more to the less *subjective.*

—But how can you prove that this modification of . . . the general viewpoint will not change its meaning?

—On that point, I can say nothing. . . .

—Now to your story: something concrete!

—You'll understand that Einstein, in order to pursue his aim, has had to form certain hypotheses. This is what I was coming to—this is where his remark comes in . . . the one I wanted to repeat to you.

—The one that so carried you away. . . .

—Nothing, nothing could have touched or affected me

more deeply. . . . At the end of his second lecture, when he had finished writing the ultimate equation, Einstein turned round to face his audience. . . . He has great charm: a rather heavy build, full, pale features, with Oriental eyes . . . black and brilliant. Something of the virtuoso; he looks a musician —there is that indefinable musical quality in his gestures and looks. And withal, completely unaffected. . . . He has a quick smile, a very ready laugh. . . . In concluding, he took care to emphasize the purely speculative character of the results which he had just been expounding. (He devoted particular care to describing a continuum *such* that the direction of *P* to the *n*th being given . . .)

—Now what's all this about?

—All right. . . . Well, what he said in the end was that there was no use looking for any experimental proof of his researches for a very long time. He seemed to be apologizing for his audacity. He took an almost coquettish and humorous delight in insisting on all the risky points in his structure. . . . And it was then that he brought in the remark that carried me away, as you put it—in the strongest . . . the aquiline or aquilean sense of the term. . . .

—Help!

—*The distance*, he said, *between the theory and its experimental proof is such that we can only estimate it from a total architectural point of view.*

—How peculiar. . . . What exactly did he mean?

—That he relied—in all conscience, with the fullest realization of what he was doing and what he was exposing himself to—on the production in his own mind. . . .

—By one of those famous leaps of yours?

—On the production—the . . . liberation of certain agreements, harmonies. On the action or intervention of certain tendencies, on the suggestion or revelation of certain symmetries, certain responses, obscure in origin and yet totally convincing. . . . What he meant was a kind of superior flair, or intuition.

—In that case, he amounts to a sort of artist, doesn't he?

—Of the very first order.

—I confess, I can't quite see how physics can be adjusted to such . . . And then again, I wonder how logic can tolerate all this inspiration and supposition.

—Don't you worry about logic. . . . Moreover, although logic can steady our progress in a certain direction, it cannot choose the direction.

—Be that as it may, there seems to me to be a lot of mysticism in all this.

—There's mysticism (since you choose to bring in the term) in everything we do which is not . . . sheer repetition! And even then! . . . But in this case it's a question of mysticism with an end in view . . . controlled, limited; used for what it is . . . the nature of the intellect supplying what the nature of things keeps hidden. Then, out of the total contribution of both natures, the sheer virtuosity of the mathematician deduces the subtlest and most unexpected results. Above all, it can do astonishing work in figures, condense relationships to an extraordinary degree. . . .

—All very pretty, said the Doctor, —but if all this labor is a fiction . . . if experience disproves it one day? . . . Then it's only a curiosity for the specialist.

—Even if it comes to nothing in the end, a task so prodigious will nonetheless have radically altered all our ideas about the nature of physics. Besides, if the content goes, the form remains. . . . What the physicist rejects can still be valued by the mathematician.

—Anyhow, whatever the outcome, your physicists are lucky. . . . In the science of living matter we're a long way from all these daring acrobatics and "architectural points of view."

—The physicists are more go-ahead than you are.

—Yes, but what a difference in the nature of the problems! . . . The further you go, the less you understand about this blessed business, *life*. . . . Its origins, requirements, and developments. . . . It's strange that of all possible things, *living* things are the most puzzling to the *living being*. . . .

—Here's a sort of corollary to your remark; it is precisely those physical properties which most resemble the properties of living substance that are least understood. Am I right?

—For example?

—Elasticity. Catalysis. Molecular dissymmetry.

—That's true enough. But what is more puzzling still is . . . how shall I put it? . . . The capriciousness, the variety, the sudden changeableness in the means which life makes use of. It plays with forces of every magnitude.

—It plays on all the chessboards at once; doesn't care whether it wins or loses, changes its choice of individual, or if need be, of race, as you'd change a shirt.

—Life's a mad thing . . . a tyrannous martyr . . . maniac, megalomaniac, frantic enough . . . to think up something like insects . . . look at a fly under the microscope. . . .

—What a nightmare! And look at Man!

—What about Woman?

—And the repetition compulsions, the echolalia of reproduction! . . . The shoals of herring!

—And a hundred million spermatozoa for one that rings the bell!

—Poor, poor little plague . . . that has to bear, from one

bank of time to another, its concentrated essence of ancestry, across the Styx of . . . Life!

—Carrying every shade of vice. . . .

—We are all upstarts. . . .

—Up to what?

—All and nothing. We're up to being . . . You . . . or Me!

—Letting the mad thing work out its delirium. . . .

—Well and truly mad. . . . It eats itself to keep alive.

—It takes a loss on every item, and wins out on the total. . . .

—Self-destructive, self-contradictory, self-confounded. . . .

—Obviously a paranoid! . . . There's no shadow of doubt.

—Doctor, you'd better take steps, at once. . . .

—The Act of 1838 makes all the necessary provisions.

—We've got to admit . . . this sorry life won't fit at all with anything we know or can conceive. What could be stupider, more elusive, crazy, obstinate? Contradictions seem to stimulate it like a drug. It insists on death, and on the instinct of survival; on toeing the line, and on being different; on a strict co-operation between economy and waste. . . .

—Do you think a man like Einstein could get out of a quandary like this?

—Would you kindly take a seat?

—For how long? One century? Or two?

—You're in an awful hurry.

—Look, here's my arm.

—What about it, Doctor? You want me to feel your pulse?

—No. Nothing. . . . I'm simply saying, here's my arm. . . . My hand.

—It's a strong square hand. . . .

—Here it is. I open it, close it, turn it about. What's inside it? An arrangement of solids: bones, levers, connecting rods, articulating sheaths . . . a fixture for . . .

—Yes. A system of "elementary" mechanisms; what is called an "apparatus."

—This apparatus is assembled and held together by ligaments. . . . So far, good. It's all quite clear.

—Yes . . . meaning to say we can construct something like it. . . .

—Agreed.

—Which means we can—in a fashion—put ourselves in the place of Nature the Engineer . . . E.C.P. Criticize it. And even improve on it sometimes.

—Yes. But wait . . . what about the forces! Let me introduce you, sir, to Mr. Muscle. We haven't invented anything like him, so far.

—Glad to meet him. In particular, Mr. Mosquito Muscle. . . . Eight thousand wingbeats per minute.

—Yes, can't you just hear them. . . . And the co-ordination of these muscles, the miraculous interlockings, the calculus of opposing forces. . . . And the way their motors are inserted. . . .

—Yes. The flexible motor, the motor integument.

—*And* the seductive, the languorous motor . . .

—What's this?

—Why, yes! The iris. Blue eyes, dark eyes. . . .

—Naughty medicine man! And anyhow, there are other muscles that ply the same charming trade . . . alas! . . .

—And don't forget the range of our motors, producing a shock one moment—a virtually explosive effect; and then an almost reversible displacement . . . movement next to motionless; and then . . . immobile for a second, seeming almost solid.

—What a masterpiece . . . it puts us in quite a quandary. But don't let's despair just yet. . . .

—Everything's been tried, more or less . . . the biological sciences are obliging enough in their way. The moment physics and chemistry catch a glimpse of something, in rush medicine and biology, drunk with anticipation. . . . Thermodynamics, batteries, piezoelectricity. . . . But then, on the other hand, irritability, contractility, tonicity—all insoluble mysteries.

—And we are still trying to find out the secret of mere rubber. . . .

—And everything acts in obedience to the nerve cell. . . . The Neuron steps on to the scene.

—Yes. And night falls on the stage. . . . Then the curtain rises on quite a different setting: The Mind, the Will . . .

—The Past, the Future, the Present. . . .

—The Implex. . . .

—And Omnivalence; and the Instincts, and Language, and Reason.

—And Unreason. . . . And all this is what works your levers. The Inconceivable sits at the end of the chain of controls governing all these simple machines. . . . The clear leads on to the obscure. Obscurity leads on to clarity.

—And behold, a connection is set up, said the Doctor, between mechanism and psyche. Nobody knows how! Still, it works . . . up to a point.

—Except in case of accident—or rheumatism.

—We've got to resign ourselves—to rheumatism . . . and to not knowing what it is. . . . We will, sometime. *Tomorrow*, perhaps? . . . I've every confidence.

—As for me, I murmured, I . . . fluctuate. When I draw up a balance sheet, I feel we can be satisfied with ourselves, and with our time. But if I look at it another way, I declare we're bankrupt. . . . If I set about adding up what we *know*, I find the gains are illusory. We have a lot of dubious currency in our accounts: and fictitious dividends are handed out with the greatest ease. . . .

—You're rather hard on us all.

—Wait. . . . If, on the other hand, I look at what we can *do*—at mankind's acquisition of real power over a century and a half, then——

—But how can you separate this fictive knowledge and this substantial power, the one from the other?

—Quite easily, my dear Doctor. In the long run, all our expectations boil down to finding *what must be done* to produce a given effect. This *doing* is all we have. And it's limited. We possess *S* senses and *M* muscles. . . . Our world is entrenched within the combined total of our perceptions and acts. We have done our best to express the total in a system of measurements—a system, that is, for establishing and repeating . . . formulas, numerical recipes. . . . A formula is nothing but a . . . mathematical prescription.

—A set of directions.

—Yes. Directions for performing . . . certain acts of measurement.

—*Fac secundum artem.*

—Yes. . . . So we have summed up in a series of formulas everything required to reproduce or foresee the phenomena under observation in the Universe according to the 1640–1850 model. . . . But research led us quickly enough outside the domain of our primitive perceptions. So we found new methods of perception and action. But these methods are indirect. They consist of *relays*. They are feelings, gropings . . . but they transpose. . . . What they indicate has to be interpreted by way of images or ideas—all borrowed perforce from our basic, invariable stock of supplies. . . .

—Unless the species evolves.

—That will take some time. . . . Meanwhile, you can see

the fix we are in. We've arrived at the bankruptcy of imagery. How imagine a world where there can be no question of seeing, touching, where there are neither figures nor categories, where the very notions of position and movement are somehow incompatible? The physicists resort to the most incredible casuistry in their efforts to escape from this. . . .

—We've gone a long way. . . . I've even been tempted to think that determinism was undermined. . . .

—Everything is. From now on, every idea has to live dangerously.

—It's a relapse, a reversion.

—No. . . . Now draw up a balance sheet in the hard currency of Science.

—What do you mean by that?

—I mean, consider simply the increase in *power*. All the rest, theories, hypotheses, analogies—mathematical or otherwise—is both indispensable and provisional. What remains as capital is simply the power of action upon things, the new achievements—the *recipes*. . . .

—You're reducing Science to the kitchen level. . . .

—My dear Doctor: one fine day Volta puts two metals into contact with an acid solution. The results are quite unheard-of. He gives them his name, and "explains" them as best he can. Today they are interpreted in quite a different fashion. In thirty years it will be different again. . . . But whether thirty or three hundred, the recipe is still sound. The theory of it may change a hundred times, the increase in man's power is always there: he still knows how to produce, by means of two metals and one acid, as defined by his senses, the means of separating water into its elements and stimulating an electromagnet. As for the cook, she's a marvel at solidifying albumen, and in the guise of *mayonnaise* she can perform colloidal feats of sleight-of-hand. . . .

—Say what you like, you're ridiculing Science. . . .

—Not at all. . . . To tell you the truth, I'm much more interested personally in the theoretical and variable side, however uncertain it may be, than in the positive acquisition of recipes, and of new powers over matter.

—Yes. And what about the sick? Do you suppose they're not affected by the acquisition of new powers over matter?

—I won't answer you. . . . Not until you've set about that History of Therapy.

—That's enough!

—A general History of Therapy . . . no! . . . A Critical and Comparative Survey of——

—Enough!

—By Doctor——

—Stop!

—Consultant to the Hospitals——

—Of Paris; don't forget *Paris.*

—True enough. Do they still make you say your lessons in front of a clock?

—A clock? . . . You mean a timer?

—Yes. A sort of taximeter.

—For the interns. And for the surgical assistants.

—So, the amount learnt by heart is counted in units of time?

—Yes. It must all be precise and to the point.

—So it's all a question of memory? . . . And what about judgment? And observation?

—No need, at that stage of learning.

—Right enough.

—Besides . . . if those qualities are not exactly looked for by the examining board, they find tremendous scope all round it, nevertheless.

—So, all in all, it's a bit like the Longchamp race track. Tipsters, trainers, and dope.

—Naturally! . . . And the results, on the average, aren't at all bad.

—I should hope so! But you'll forgive a superficial observer if he's slightly . . . surprised.

—Surprise, my dear man, always comes of contrasting what is not with what is.

—Oh, very well. . . . And it looks as if night was on the point of surprising you and me.

—True. Look at that sky. . . . Perfect. Not a cloud.

—The sun seems to be set low on a pillar of fire, and the rest of the sea's all pearl. . . .

—Just about time to think of going. If the dark came down, you could easily break a leg among these rocks.

—My eyes are dazzled with fire . . . and yet haunted by a glorious blue-green.

—That's a healthy retinal response.

—It's a little like . . . an *idée fixe.*

—Excellent! . . .

—And now I see nothing but green.

—Close your eyes.

—The tighter I close them the more I see. . . . Green, crimson, powder-blue, pink . . .

—The whole gamut. . . .

—Before returning to its equilibrium, my optical implex runs through all its repertoire. . . .

—Confidentially, my friend, you've been up to the same thing yourself. . . .

—You're very good. I'm afraid I've talked a lot of nonsense. . . .

—Tut, tut. . . .

—It was just what I most needed.

—A consultation?

—No. Treatment.

—At my expense?

—What do you suppose?

—Oh, I can see there's something wrong. But I won't ask questions. For all the fashionable notions, I persist in the conviction that there are glomerules of resentment, tangles of worry, that are better not teased out.

—Yes. . . . *Inquieta non movere.*

—All depends on the individual. And you are one of those individuals who offer the most difficult line of approach. You are a mine of potential . . . defenses. I wager that the slightest touch——

—Less than . . . even the threat of a touch, and I want to howl . . . I feel ready to faint.

—Exactly. How nicely arranged! Physically and morally you are all of a piece. . . . I can tell that at a glance.

—And what do you see?

—A nervous, ravaged expression—an *immediate* face, I would call it, with a strange mixture of young and old in it. . . . You can read every tense of the verb "to be" in it . . . all active at once. You have a physiognomy full of incident; and your eye, it's either more alert or more remote than it should be. . . . Do you know what you make me think of? . . . You'll forgive the comparison; it occurs irresistibly, somehow. And anyway, you haven't been overconsiderate yourself.

—Don't stand on ceremony. . . . But don't say any of those things that keep coming back, to ferment, and to be brooded over in the mind. . . . I don't need any more mental . . . nettle-stings, I assure you.

—Have you read *Notre Dame de Paris*?

—Hugo? About . . . a hundred years ago.

—Me, too. But one thing I remember. . . . Do you recall the weird exercise in light-fingered robbery which the tramps and pickpockets carry out in the Cour des Miracles?

—I don't see the point.

—The thieving gentry put themselves in training by trying to abstract a purse from a strung-up dummy, sewn all over with little bells and shivering trinkets. A tricky business. At the slightest stir, the hanged figure responds—with musical chimes! And the game's up.

—But the same tale comes in Dickens, in *Oliver Twist*. . . . Dickens must have stolen it from Hugo. . . .

—Without ringing a single bell.

—Unless they both . . .

—It can happen.

—But what has all this to do with me? I've never plundered anyone; and if anyone else has been through my pockets, I never gave a murmur.

—All the same (and this is why I mentioned that story) . . . I can see you hung all over with . . . nervous little bells. The slightest breath, and you react with a whole carillon of notions and responses.

—Poor me. . . .

—Wait! And then you react against these reactions in an altogether peculiar way. . . .

—Go on, go on. What's the sentence?

—You react, you fight back with abstractions, a whole orgy of precisions and definitions. Intellectual concentration acts as your insulator. . . .

—Crusoe's island. . . .

—Yes, Crusoe's island. I see that. You know, my friend,

when you set about a series of propositions aimed—for instance—at destroying the whole notion of an *idée fixe* . . . or, on a bigger scale, when you try, with the help of arguments that are obviously biased, personal, clearly affective in origin, to dismiss the already very respectable fabric of what we've achieved in the way of intellectual research . . . I can only say, in my own little corner of a mind, that you're doing a bit of special pleading. There are theories that can look . . . oh, so impersonal—but they flash a very lively portrait of a gentleman on to the screen.

—You're all too lucid, Doctor.

—Oh, I'm not being clever. It's an absolute rule, where psychology's concerned: never be too clever.

—But surely——

—It's an obvious "must." Never try to get inside a patient's mental setup.

—Because you'd never get out again?

—The spitefulness of the sick, God help us, is . . .

—Quite insensate.

—Inconceivable. So don't put silly ideas into my head. It just will not do to try to follow them into the subjective labyrinths they build themselves. . . . Now, as far as you are concerned, all I need do is watch you talk, listen to your tone, the excitement in your voice. The way people talk tells you more than what they say. . . . The content in itself has no . . . essential importance.

—Odd. That's one theory of poetry. And it even applies . . .

—To what?

—I went rather far, one day. But I won't dare repeat what I said. . . . No matter.

—Tell me.

—I told a group of philosophers to their faces: "Philosophy is simply a question of form."

—Now that was an unkind cut. . . . You should take care of your responses.

—But it wasn't a case of response. . . . It simply occurred to me as obvious.

—And did they react? Kick up a fuss?

—Not at all. They thought it over, or they seemed to.

—If I'd been they . . . But to go back to what I was telling you. The content of what is said amounts, nine times out of ten, only to what I call routine automatic invention.

—To talk is to create; but what is so created has exactly the same propensity for dying as it had for being born.

—Maybe so. But this almost continuous invention of talk grows less and less automatic as circumstances call for more and more specialized adaptation. . . . A man with a gun who does nothing but fire his weapon at random is indulging in automatic emission. But if he has to hit an agreed target, and if that target is moving, or replaceable . . .

—That's why I came down among these rocks.

—How do you mean?

—To carry out an exercise in specialized adaptation at every step.

—But what for?

—To break a cycle. To force myself to invent at every single instant some new, fairly difficult, and always unforeseen act or other.

—Not a bad idea.

—You think so too? I had already found that walking on the level simply exasperated what was . . . exasperating me. You can walk on the flat as though your body didn't exist. You can shoot along, stop short—entirely possessed by the rhythm of your thoughts. They drag you, whip you along, or nail you to the spot. . . . It's like a crippled boat, at the wind's mercy——

—The compass gone crazy, and the helm smashed. . . . Tell me, how've you been sleeping?

—Not at all for three weeks.

—Holy Moses! You'll just have to take something.

—Doctor, let's be off. You can scarcely see your hand in front of you. The lighthouses have been sweeping the sector for a quarter of an hour now.

—Off we go!

—It was good of you to stand my company for this long. I . . . hardly knew how I was going to live through this afternoon. Thanks to you . . .

—Why not have dinner together?

—Oh . . .

—We could go to the cinema.

—You loathe films.

—Yes. But you can always smoke.

—But I don't want to. . . .

—Look. You take the basket, I'll carry the painting gear. . . . Don't you see, I'm a moral creature. I'm not going to let you out of my sight, not with all these complications. And then, don't forget I've that disease of activity. . . . Come along, up this way.

—Thanks. But really——

—I'm telling you, I'm not going to let you go. . . . A man on his own is always in bad company.

NOTES

NOTES

THESE NOTES are limited, with a few exceptions, to clarifying the allusions and other sorts of references that a French reader might be expected to catch but an American or English reader might not. In the bibliographical headnote, the place of publication is always Paris.

David Paul, the translator, is an English critic and poet. He has translated two other volumes in the Collected Works: *Degas, Manet, Morisot* and the Faust plays.

I have drawn freely and gratefully, as before, on Professor Jean Hytier's notes to the Pléiade edition of Valéry, and on his own kindness for further details.

Miss Paula Deitz is the true maker of these Notes. I am happily indebted to her for her generous and resourceful collaboration. To Mme. Catherine David also, for suggestions arising from her perceptive critical reading of the manuscript. To Mrs. Diane Amussen for the scope and sensitiveness of her editing. And to Mr. Jeremy Bernstein for reviewing the scientific terms in the passages from Valéry's Notebooks (pp. 120 ff.).

J. M.

IDÉE FIXE: *A Duologue by the Sea*: L'IDÉE FIXE, *ou Deux Hommes à la Mer*.

Valéry evidently wrote this dialogue in the fall of 1931; he read it to Gide in manuscript on January 5, 1932 (see pp. x f.).

The first edition, limited to 300 copies, was published by a pharmaceutical firm, Les Laboratoires Martinet, "exclusively for the medical profession"; it was printed and produced by Robert Lang, March 10, 1932. A second limited edition of 640 copies was published by *La Nouvelle Revue française* in 1933.

The author's foreword "To the Reader," under the heading *Au lecteur de cette nouvelle édition*, made its appearance in the first trade edition, *N.R.F.*, 1934. The subtitle, *Deux Hommes à la Mer*, was dropped from this edition but was restored by Julien P. Monod in *Œuvres*, Volume F, *N.R.F.*, 1936. See *Œuvres II*, Pléiade (1960).

The phrase *deux hommes à la mer* makes a fairly untranslatable play on words, meaning either "two men overboard" or "two men by the sea," or rather both at once, as Valéry no doubt intended. David Paul has rightly found his own solution.

L'Idée Fixe was written in haste, as Valéry says. It was also published in haste, with the result that the first edition contained a number of textual inaccuracies—an occasional wrong attribution of speeches, mistaken words (*philoclassiques* for *philoclastiques*, p. 84), and plain typographical errors. Most of these have remained in all subsequent editions of the French text, but have been set to rights, I believe, in so far as they affect the translation.

Two excerpts from *L'Idée Fixe* have been previously published in English: the first translated by Eleanor Wolff, *Mesa*, No. 2, Autumn, 1946; the other by Herbert Steiner and Eleanor Wolff, *Etc.*, Chicago, Autumn, 1948.

7. *En roscas de cristal serpiente breve*: the first line of Góngora's poem *De la Toma de Larache* (1610–11), which begins:

> *En roscas de cristal serpiente breve,*
> *Por la arena desnuda el Luco yerra . . .*
>
> In crystal coils a small serpent,
> The Luco [river] winds through the naked sand . . .

14. *What the Pre-Raphaelites called "An Entire Adherence to the Simplicity of Nature"*: "ce que les préraphaélites appelaient: Une entière adhérence à la simplicité de la nature." The quotation is from the statement of principles written by W. M. Rossetti for the first number of the Pre-Raphaelites' monthly review, *The Germ* (Jan. 1850).

15. "*You are a physician, Doctor, and in pain!*": "Vous êtes médecin, docteur, et vous souffrez." The French parodies a famous line from Racine's *Bérénice* (IV, 5): "Vous êtes empereur, Seigneur, et vous pleurez!" (You are the Emperor, my Lord, and you weep!)

My friend, a doctor feels it more than most: This line in French, "Le médecin, mon cher, souffre plus que quiconque," is an absurd Alexandrine responding to the take-off on Racine just above, and justifying the retort of *similia similibus* and "doggerel" in the next line.

Similia similibus . . .: The complete phrase, *similia similibus curentur* (like may be cured by like), states the principle of homeopathic medicine: that diseases may be cured by drugs which produce in a healthy person symptoms similar to those of the disease itself. This system of therapeutics was introduced in 1796 by a German physician, Samuel Hahnemann (1755–1843), though the principle had been anticipated by Hippocrates and Paracelsus. It has been corroborated, according to the homeopathists, by modern serum therapy, which treats even the most malignant diseases (lockjaw, typhoid fever, tuberculosis) by introducing into the body a modified form of the poisons that produce them.

The tenet of classical medicine is the opposite: *contraria contrariis curantur* (contraries are cured by their contraries).

22. *Can last only a moment*: "ne dure qu'un instant." In this passage Valéry is playing something like a refrain on a line from a popular eighteenth-century love song, *Plaisir d'Amour*. It begins:

> *Plaisir d'amour ne dure qu'un moment,*
> *Chagrin d'amour dure toute la vie.*
>
> The pleasure of love lasts but a moment,
> The sorrow of love endures a lifetime.

The song is the work of the German conductor and composer J. P. E. Martini (1741–1816), professor at the Paris Conservatory and superintendent of music at the French court. Berlioz once made an arrangement of it.

23. *A moralist . . . or an immoralist*: "en moraliste . . . ou en immoraliste," doubtless a sly reference to Gide and his novel *L'Immoraliste*.

A not very readable writer. . . . I forget his name: Valéry is of course referring to himself. The passage he cites is from *Rhumbs*. (See Collected Works, Vol. 14.)

The lady should have married a dancer; and instead she fell to a computer: "Il fallait un danseur à Madame; ce fut un calculateur qui l'obtint!" Valéry has taken a line from Beaumarchais' *Mariage de Figaro* (V, 3), and inverted it. Beaumarchais: "il fallait un calculateur, etc. . . ."

To give and to withhold is not . . .: "Donner et retenir ne vaut . . . ," a term from old French law which might be translated in more or less legal terms as "a gift is not complete without delivery."

24. *A good supper, a good bed, and . . . this other thing*: "Bon souper, bon gîte, et ce reste," one of Valéry's favorite lines from La Fontaine (*Fables*, IX, 2, "Les Deux Pigeons"). He has altered it slightly (*ce reste* for *le reste*) to point the implication:

> *Mon frère a-t-il tout ce qu'il veut,*
> *Bon soupé, bon gîte, et le reste?*
>
> Does my brother have all that he needs,
> A good supper, a good bed, and the rest?

25. *Stegomyia*: the yellow-fever mosquito.

28. *The air's so clear, the sea's so . . . wide*: "L'air est pur, la mer est . . . large." Valéry is playing with a line from Paul Déroulède's popular poem "Le Clairon" (*Chants du soldat*, 1872).

> *L'air est pur, la route est large,*
> *Le clairon sonne la charge . . .*
>
> The air is clear, the road is wide,
> The trumpet sounds the charge . . .

Déroulède (1846–1914): patriot, politician, and poet.

32. *Principiis obsta*: "resist the beginnings," the motto of preventive medicine, from Ovid's *Remedia amoris* (*The Remedies for Love*):

> *Principiis obsta; sero medicina paratur,*
> *Cum mala per longas convaluere moras.*
>
> Fight the disease at the start, for once the symptoms develop,
> Medicine comes too late, losing effect from delay.
>
> (Tr. by Rolfe Humphries.)

Quieta non movere . . . : "Do not disturb what is quiet," or "Let sleeping dogs lie." (See *Inquieta non movere*, p. 104 & *n*.)

I won't take your bet. Any more than I'll take Pascal's . . .: the reference is of course to Pascal's famous wager on the existence of God. (See his *Pensées*, Everyman edition, Section III: "Of the Necessity of the Wager.")

Chorda dorsalis: the notochord, or spinal cord.

33. . . . *Whether neutral or . . . helpful. . . . What a piece of neutromania!*: "Vagues ou . . . sympathiques! . . . C'est une formule de vagotonie! . . ."

The French text here is a complex play on words, involving both ordinary and technical meanings. In physiology and medicine, *vague* and *sympathique* are opposed terms: *vague* referring to the reactions of the vagus (parasympathetic) nerves; *sympathique*, to the reactions of the sympathetic nervous system. *La vagotonie* (Eng. "vagotonia") is a condition of nervousness and fatigue resulting from irritation of the vagus nerves.

The Doctor is saying in effect that Valéry's state of *vagotonia* is what makes him talk so much and say such odd things. No direct translation of this complex of meanings is possible. David Paul has created an equivalent play in different terms.

38. *I am always living two years ahead*: "Je ne vis jamais que dans deux ans," a remark of Napoleon's, often cited by Valéry. (See Collected Works, Vol. 7, p. 36 & *n.*, and Vol. 10, p. 388 & *n.*)

41. *Trice*: "tourne-main." Valéry is wryly disapproving of the journalistic use of a somewhat affected archaic term *tourne-main* for the correct modern form *tour de main*.

Pronounce, O king . . .: "Achevez, Seigneur." A sort of stock phrase from French classical drama.

Athaliah's dream: A passage from Racine, learned by heart in French schools (*Athalie*, II, 5). (See Collected Works, Vol. 10, p. 5.)

42. *That reason knoweth not*: "Que la raison ne connaît pas," an allusion to the most widely known of all Pascal's dicta: "Le cœur a ses raisons, que la raison ne connaît point" (The heart has its reasons, that reason knows nothing of).

46. *Edmond T.*: Edmond Teste is the proper name of Valéry's alter ego, Monsieur Teste (Mr. Head). (See Collected Works, Vol. 6.)

49. *Poor us!*: "Pauvres de nous!" Valéry's phrase is a local turn of speech from his native region, the South of France.

52. *Inspirational deficiency*: "insuffisance pithiatique." The French phrase is another case of Valéry's familiarity with medical terminology. *Insuffisance* is the pathological condition of a tissue or an organ unable to perform all its normal functions. *Pithiatique* (*pithiatisme*) is a term originated by Babinski (see note for p. 70) to designate those forms of hysteria curable by hypnotic suggestion. The unlikely combination of the two terms is the point of the passage.

Creative Ignorance: "C'est l'Ignorance Créatrice." The capitalization indicates that in French the words are meant to recall Bergson's *L'Évolution Créatrice*.

55–63. *Robinson Crusoe and his parrots*: In this long passage and at points throughout the rest of the dialogue, Valéry sketches a wry portrait of himself as a kind of "Crusoe of the intellect," shooting down parrots, i.e., meaningless words, from the sky of the mind.

Robinson Crusoe was a figure of large human meaning for Valéry. In one of his prose poems he develops it into a penetrating study of the human potential—a study that is at once a self-portrait and a portrait of man. (See "Crusoe, Idle, Pensive, Well Set Up," Collected Works, Vol. 2; also Vol. 10, p. 38.)

59. "*Sunspot*": "tache jaune," literally, the "yellow spot," or *macula lutea*, an oval depression at the back of the retina.

Fovea centralis: the center of the oval depression (*macula lutea*) and the eye's point of acutest vision.

As this whole passage demonstrates, Valéry thought of the eye almost as the "organ of consciousness," and had studied its anatomy and functions in detail.

62. *And what about . . . the rest? . . . The rest is silence? . . . let's forget about how to deal with the rest*: "Et . . . le reste? . . . Le reste est silence? . . . Laissons l'art d'accommoder le reste . . ."

Valéry doesn't stick at triple fooling, bringing together "The Two Pigeons" (see note for p. 24), with Hamlet's last words, and a phrase from French kitchen talk. "L'art d'accommoder *les restes*" means "how to deal with leftovers" from the dining table.

68. *Hope . . . is the heart's best gift from heaven*: "L'espoir . . . il est vrai nous soulage . . ." The first line of a silly poem used by Molière for ridicule, in *Le Misanthrope* (I, 2): "Hope comforts us a while, 'tis true." (Tr. by Richard Wilbur.)

69. *Oportet haereses esse*: "For there must be also heresies." I Corinthians 11:19 (A. V.).

"*Mechanics*": "Méchanique." In French, Valéry uses the eighteenth-century spelling of the title of Barthez's treatise, which "dates" his work. (The modern French spelling is *mécanique*.)

Barthez: Paul Joseph Barthez (1734–1806) grew up in Montpellier, Valéry's home, and became one of that city's most distinguished citizens, Chancellor of the university there and later a member of the Institut de France. He wrote a number of works on the science of man, among them his masterpiece, *Nouvelle Méchanique des Mouvements de l'homme et des animaux* (1798).

70. *Babinski*: Joseph Babinski (1857–1932), French neurologist, known mainly for his work on disorders of the nervous system. He transformed the conception of hysteria, confining

it to those symptoms which can be provoked or suppressed by suggestion (*pithiatisme*). (See note for p. 52.)

Foix: Charles Foix (1882–1927), French neurologist. His major work was the study of clinical and anatomical disturbances in vascular diseases.

Froment: Jules Froment (1878–1946), a French neurologist who worked with Babinski on the hysteria syndrome.

75. *What on earth did you think you were doing, going into politics?*: "Que diable alliez-vous faire dans la politique?" The French here echoes a line every Frenchman knows, from Molière's *Fourberies de Scapin* (II, 7): "Que diable allait-il faire dans cette galère?" (What the deuce was he doing in that galley?)

76. *I'm as sure of myself as I am of . . . You are of the Universe*: "Je suis maître de moi comme de l'Univers . . ." (I am master of myself as I am of the whole world). In French the two talkers are playing with a memorable line spoken by the Emperor Augustus in Corneille's *Cinna* (V, 3). (See also Collected Works, Vol. 13, p. 26 & *n*.)

79. *Sovereign Good*: For Valéry "Our Sovereign Good" is of course the Mind. See his essay "Politics of the Mind," which in French carries the subtitle, *Notre Souverain Bien* (Collected Works, Vol. 10).

82. *One trousered lady breeds a thousandfold*: "Un pantalon pour dame en fait paraître mille . . ." Valéry's line here parodies another memorable Alexandrine spoken by Augustus in Corneille's *Cinna* (IV, 2):

> *Rome a pour ma ruine une hydre trop fertile:*
> *Une tête coupée en fait renaître mille.*
>
> Rome for my ruin doth a hydra hold:
> One severed head can breed a thousandfold.
> (Tr. by David Paul)

84. *Philoclastic*: The French text has "philoclassiques," surely a misprint for "philoclastiques." (David Paul's emendation.)

87. *Napoleon? So we're always coming back to him . . .* : The French here is "Napoléon? . . . lui, toujours lui . . . ," an allusion to the title and first line of one of Victor Hugo's earliest poems on Napoleon. The poem, *Lui*, begins: "Toujours lui! Lui partout!" (*Les Orientales*, 1829.) (See p. 38 & *n.*)

89. *Cuvier*: Georges Cuvier (1769–1832), French naturalist, founder of comparative anatomy and paleontology. Cuvier was the first scientist to reconstruct certain unknown species on the basis of a few fossil bones. He believed in the immutability of species, and fought the evolutionist theories of his time. His principal works: *Leçons d'anatomie comparée* (1800–05), *Recherches sur les ossements fossiles* (1812), *Le Règne animal distribué d'après son organisation* (1817).

91. *About two years ago Einstein*: This passage lightly disguises Valéry's true interest in the man and his work. The Notebooks refer to special relativity theory as early as 1906. In 1919 he translated an article on general relativity from the London *Athenaeum* for publication in the *Nouvelle Revue française* (Dec. 1, 1919). From 1918–22 the Notebooks show his growing interest in the geometry of the subject; and in February 1923 he was reading Einstein's *Meaning of Relativity* (1922). (See Judith Robinson, "Language, Physics and Mathematics in Valéry's Cahiers," *Modern Language Review*, Oct. 1960, p. 519; see also Collected Works, Vol. 13, pp. 282–3.)

When Einstein came to Paris in November 1929 for a series of lectures and conferences, Valéry attended his lectures (Nov. 9 and 12) and later took him to call on Bergson, at a clinic where Bergson was undergoing treatment. The following selections from the Notebooks for this period will give some sense of the impact Einstein's visit had on him.

9 Nov. 5:30. Einstein's lecture. Einstein old, heavy.
Speaks very slowly, with an accent, and long pauses.
At first nothing difficult—then—few understand.
He lays out his scheme—unity of nature—to find the simplest laws.

* * *

To make gravitation a property of space is all very well. But that does not change our knowledge of gravitation as a phenomenon—which remains *shut, occult*. That is to say that the nature of matter (which is something we *imagine*) does not force such knowledge upon the imagination. Nothing seems to *illustrate* the action of matter on matter—Etc.

But in the idea of relativity it is rather the contrary—it is space that is modified. For between the 2 notions—space and gravity (or space and matter)—it is space that is *deduced, constructed*; the other is *observed*. Yet in the theory it is the *second* that is modified, since it is the second that is elastic . . .

This is a general fact: when two notions, taken together, differ in variability, the one least accessible to experience is the one that varies, under the influence of the mind.

* * *

The past is the *sensation* that a certain event or object could not be found by the quickest possible search of the whole sphere of our *sustained* sensations.

* * *

The meaning of a sentence is the resultant of all the mutual deformations of the immediate (reflex) meanings of the separate words,
from contact and from the valences of position and inflexion.
(Example: A sentence spoken word by word, at long intervals.)

Einstein is searching for the simplest and most natural laws, as the meaning of the physical universe.

Each separate law is a *word*, etc.

We do as he does in every sentence.

Sentence—a group of words whose meanings undergo reciprocal deformation.

Certain words deform their neighbors without being deformed—prepositions, conjunctions. (N.B. Adverbs are invariable but not necessarily.)

So what may happen is that the component terms may simultaneously cancel each other out: $\Sigma m = o$.

But there is something else that is not canceled: $S = \Sigma s$.

* * *

Anybody's relative naïveté.

Einstein's naïveté, Bergson's naïveté.

The special naïveté of men who attempt to set up a kind of structure that will include everything.

It is the *everything* that constitutes their naïveté. I know what it's like.

* * *

Impression from Einstein's lecture—

We know how to *write* what we do not know.

Write the form (circumscribe) the intelligible conditions—

Write what ought to be—the form of the law that would express the unity of physical nature.

It's a kind of metrics.

In a way it's a regression counter to the separation of the senses.

We can perceive an incoherent whole.

* * *

11 Nov. Long conversation with Bergson, about 6 o'clock. His idea of life is curious. He always contrasts life with "matter," and thinks the aim or law of life is to produce *unexpected acts.* I didn't want to pursue the idea, which he tells me came to him from considering everything that distinguishes life . . . etc.

We talked aesthetics, in connection with a book he had in his hand—R. Rolland's *Beethoven*. He said that what R. R. says about the "architecture" in Beethoven surprised him (making Beethoven a less sentimental creator than anyone thought), and that it seemed to make Beethoven more like me. I developed my own idea, since he spoke of my "intellectualism." I told him not to be mistaken, that I am a *formiste*—and that the fact of beginning with forms, going from the form to the "matter" of works or ideas, gives the *impression* of intellectualism, by analogy with logic—but that forms are intuitive in origin—and I told him about my theory of ornament: the formation by the sensibility of something to fill a vacancy, following local-general laws (contrasts and symmetries.)

He asked me, several times, whether I agree with what Gillouin says about my sonnet *Grenades*.

* * *

I "see" a whole calculus of the possibilities of "consciousness."

It would require first those *absolute* definitions I am always trying to find, whose aim and end it is to relate everything that happens to its real and immediate variables.

An *instant* is an *n-tuplet*.

Out of this *n*-tuplet *may* come a group of transformations.

Some of these retain it, others change it.

* * *

The basic elements of knowledge are not special sensations, etc., but awareness, surprise, expectation, relaxed attention, recognition, impulse, restraints, too fast, too slow, too strong, too weak, more, enough, already, etc.

* * *

12 Nov. Louis de Broglie's lecture—Sorbonne—It strikes me as a total confusion of ideas. 37 years ago I made up my mind about these obscure matters—by distinguishing purely and simply between an image, an observation, a sign, etc.—I very frankly congratulate myself!

Discussion—Einstein—Borel—Langevin—etc. Xavier Léon presiding, beckons to me to speak—No, says my head. I don't know enough about the matter to make my idea fit precisely into what is being said—

I spoke of this to Cartan as we were walking up toward the Poincaré Institute. Scientists are disconcerted when someone refers Science back to absolute axes.

5:30 Einstein's lecture.

I was very much interested toward the end—He showed himself to be a great artist, and he's the only *artist* among all these scientists. He talked about his uncertainty and his *faith* founded on the architecture (or beauty) of forms. This struck home to me. Einstein can operate as I would have liked to do—by way of *forms.*

Einstein: "The distance between reality and theory is such that we have to take architectural points of view." Nothing could have given me more pleasure to hear, nothing confirms me more in my own ideas, since in the domain of ψ φ [mind-matter] it is millions of times more true than in the domain of φ [matter].

D'Ocagne told me confidentially that Picaud (at the meeting in the Academy of Sciences, with Einstein present) refused to allow Borel to introduce Einstein to him (because he's German). This is despicable.

97. *The Act of 1838*: The first French law regulating the segregation and care of the insane, passed June 30, 1838.

98. *E.C.P.*: École Centrale de Paris, the National Engineering School.

100. *Fac secundum artem*: "Work by the rules of the art."

Relays: Valéry has in mind the figure of a broken-circuit relay for the indirect transmission of energy. For his repeated use of this figure, see Collected Works, Vol. 12, p. 38 & *n.*; Vol. 13, p. 39 & *n.*, etc.

103. *The whole gamut*: The French text here is *Toute la lyre* ("the whole sweep of the lyre"). Valéry uses the phrase as the familiar expression it is, but he no doubt had in the back of his mind at least two of its literary uses: as the title of the two last collections of Victor Hugo's poems, drawn from every period of his career and published after his death (1888 and 1893); and as a figurative comment on Fanny's sensuality, in Alphonse Daudet's *Sapho* (ch. III).

104. *Inquieta non movere*: "Do not disturb what is already unquiet"—the reverse of the expression used earlier (p. 32 & *n.*).

105. *Go on, go on. What's the sentence?*: "Achève, et prends ma vie après . . ." Valéry's line is from a speech by Don Diègue in Corneille's *Le Cid* (I, 3):

> *Achève, et prends ma vie après un tel affront,*
> *Le premier dont ma race ait vu rougir son front.*
>
> Draw and kill me after this cold shame,
> The first disgrace that ever marked my name.
> (Tr. by James Schevill)

This colophon was chosen from a number of drawings by Paul Valéry of his favorite device.

GPSR Authorized Representative: Easy Access System Europe - Mustamäe tee 50, 10621 Tallinn, Estonia, gpsr.requests@easproject.com

www.ingramcontent.com/pod-product-compliance
Lightning Source LLC
LaVergne TN
LVHW050609070826
845179LV00021B/223

* 9 7 8 0 6 9 1 2 9 2 8 6 1 *